UNHOLY GODS

WILLIAM LONG

SEVERED**PRESS**

UNHOLY GODS

For Agnes

Whether beyond the stormy Hebrides,
Where thou perhaps under the whelming tide
Visit'st the bottom of the monstrous world.

John Milton
1638

ONE

The third sign shall be the birds.
From an ancient Hebridean prophecy.

Wallace Psychiatric Hospital stood like a forgotten castle in the Scottish countryside. The hospital was surrounded by ancient trees that loomed over each other, each casting a shadow much taller than itself. Hills rolled away from the woods until they met the horizon. Fields stretched for several miles in every direction before they eventually transformed into farmland. The hospital was a private and peaceful place, tucked away and hidden from the outside world. It was the perfect place for a patient to overcome their trauma.

Amongst the trees, a yellow car drove up the long meandering driveway towards the hospital. The sun hadn't risen high enough to illuminate the road yet and wouldn't for a few more hours. The car's headlights weren't bright enough to shine into the woods, and only just managed to light up the road ahead before it made another sharp turn.

Anne Jackson looked out of the window as she drove. She had to crane her neck to see the top of the trees. Firs and pines on either side of her turned the narrow road into a dark corridor. Birds circled high above her, looking over the land. To her right, she caught a glimpse of a deer in the woods. It hopped away, flashing its white Bambi-tail, and disappeared into the mossy darkness before Anne could focus her eyes on it. As she drove nearer to the hospital the trees made way for grassy banks. Bundles of rabbits huddled together, filling their chubby cheeks with grass whilst keeping a watchful eye out for foxes and other predators hiding in the dark.

Anne watched a handful of younger rabbits hop away as the car approached them. 'I wouldn't mind spending some time here, myself,' she muttered. She wound down the windows to let the fresh country air breeze through her car. She breathed in deeply, filling her lungs. The oxygen felt different here. It felt pure.

Anne parked her car at the end of the driveway. The hospital was much taller up close. The large sandstone bricks stretched high above Anne as they curved to frame grand arched windows. There were four round turrets on this side of the hospital: two either side of the main entrance, and two on the far corners of the building, making her feel like she had stepped back in time to the Middle Ages.

Anne got out of her car and removed her bag from the boot. As soon as she locked the car she was hit by quietness. She lived on the high street of a small village and was used to the constant drone of local traffic out of her window. There wasn't the sound of any vehicle this deep into the country. Instead, she heard the songs of the birds, the gentle whispers of the trees in the breeze, and not much else.

She pressed the buzzer on the front door. At first, she thought it was broken because it didn't make a noise, but once a tinny voice spoke to her through the speakers, she realised that even the buzzer was silent. They really were trying to provide a sense of tranquillity for their patients. Any unwanted noise might hinder the healing process.

'Hello?' the voice asked, crackling like a busted radio.

'Hi. Anne Jackson. I'm the hairdresser,' she said.

The speaker cut out and she heard the door click as it unlocked. She pushed open the doors.

The reception area was decorated in dark wood. There was a seating area by an unlit fireplace, with leather sofas and a coffee table. A water dispenser bubbled next to a shelf of the hospital's literature, with pamphlets about their treatments, programs, and costs. It reminded her of an old camping lodge, the kind of lodge where aristocracy might have found themselves retreating from the city a few hundred years ago.

The tall woman at reception called her over. Her face was long and pale, with deep wrinkles folding beneath her cheeks and eyes that drooped like a blood hound. Her casual demeanour made Anne think that she'd been working here for a long time. She dropped a clipboard in front of Anne and handed her a pen. It had a reassuring weight to it.

'Can you sign in please?' the receptionist said.

Anne signed her name on the sign-in sheet and dated it with the day's date.

'Where's Cheryl?' the receptionist asked.

'Did they not say, when they called?' Anne asked. 'I'm covering for her whilst she recovers.'

'Recovers?' She scrunched up her face.

'She was in a car crash,' Anne told her. 'Broke her neck.'

'Oh dear,' the receptionist said as she stroked her own neck. 'How terrible. She normally cuts my hair too when she comes...' She lingered on the last word, waiting for Anne to catch on.

'Oh, I don't mind cutting your hair for you, if you'd like?' Anne said.

'I'll wait to see how well you cut the patients' hair, and then let you know before you leave,' she said with a smile and winked one of her droopy eyes. She handed Anne a visitor's badge with her name printed on it and Anne took it and clipped it to her blouse.

Anne looked around her. There were several doors and corridors leading from the reception area. Each one headed to somewhere deep within the hospital. She turned back to the receptionist and asked, 'Which way do I go?'

The receptionist looked up, as if she were surprised that Anne didn't know the place as well as she did. She nodded with her head and said, 'Room 139. Just go down there and follow the signs, dear.'

Anne followed the directions and walked down a long corridor. She looked cautiously around her, unsure of what to expect. Nurses and patients crossed paths in front of her. The reception area felt like walking into a stately home, but the rest of the building felt more like an actual hospital. This was her first time in a psychiatric hospital, so she was a little unsure as to how she should behave and who she could and couldn't talk to. She decided that she'd only talk to patients who came in for a haircut. That felt like the safest thing for her to do.

She wasn't sure what psychiatric hospitals were supposed to look like, she'd only ever seen them in films and on TV. Art hung on the walls. It was primarily landscape paintings of fields, lakes, and wildlife; art designed to make you feel calm. Occasionally the artwork depicted something a little more action-packed, like a young man fishing from a still pond or a shepherd napping in a field with his dog.

Anne peered through an open door, into a patient's room, and was surprised to see that it looked rather cosy and not as much like a sterile hospital room as she had expected. There were framed photos, a colourful rug, and even a stuffed, cuddly walrus sitting atop a bundle of soft blankets on the bed, waiting for the patient to return.

After wandering the halls for a few minutes, she finally found her room. It had a small wooden plaque with the number 139 painted in gold. Beneath it there was a sheet of cream, watermarked paper with the word 'Haircuts' printed on it. Beneath that was a sheet with names and times for patients to sign up to get their hair cut. Every single slot had already been filled.

'It's going to be a busy day,' Anne said beneath her breath as she opened the door. When she walked into the room she saw that it had been made up for her. There were six chairs on one side of the room, creating a little waiting area, and a sink and mirror on the other side. Beside the sink was a stack of white, pillowy towels.

Anne unpacked her bag and laid out her tools next to the sink. She had her clippers, her combs, her hair products – everyone deserves to feel good about their hair – and her pride and joy: a pair of golden hair scissors with a flying mallard engraved onto the blade. It was a gift from her father for completing her diploma and getting her first job in a salon. He had always been supportive of her and had even grown a beard for her to practice on when he found out that beard grooming was going to be a part of her final assessment. The scissors were a constant reminder of how much he had done for her. Those memories were precious to her now that he was gone.

She checked the signup sheet. Her first appointment was in twenty minutes. She took a deep breath and relaxed herself before wandering back out into the halls. She found the cafeteria and bought herself a cup of tea.

'It's just like cutting anyone else's hair,' she murmured as she stirred a packet of sugar into her tea. 'You're going to be fine.'

TWO

You will see the shedding of blood.
From an ancient Hebridean prophecy.

John Calvary signed up to have his hair cut before lunch. It had become a simple pleasure for him. Even at his age, he liked to keep up his appearance. Getting a haircut always seemed to give him a pleasant little mood-boost. It hadn't always been like that. When he was younger it was just something that needed to be done. But when he first started work, and began to take pride in how he looked, his monthly haircuts made him feel good. Now that he was much older, and spent his days at Wallace Psychiatric Hospital, he looked forward to his haircuts even more.

John knocked on the door above the sign-up sheet.

'Come in,' Anne said.

Anne smiled at John as he walked into the room and closed the door behind him. She was much younger than Cheryl, who usually cut his hair, and dressed a little nicer too. The nurses weren't telling the patients why Anne had come instead of Cheryl, but John overheard two nurses whispering about the car crash whilst they were walking past his room.

I hope Cheryl's okay, John thought. He enjoyed their monthly chats. She had the ability to make him forget where he was, even if it was just for half an hour.

'Hi,' John said. 'I think I've got the appointment after Sam.'

Anne was cutting the hair of Sam Locke. Sam was a former soldier in his late twenties who had been suffering from post-traumatic stress disorder ever since he returned from his tour. Sam didn't talk about his time in the army, not with John at least, but John hoped that he spoke about it with the counsellors and psychotherapists the hospital employed.

'Hi Sam,' John said.

'How you doing?' Sam asked. He seemed down today. Like anyone, the patients here had good days and bad days. The only difference was that a bad day here could get you an extra hour of counselling and three to four more pills in your little plastic cup.

'Same as ever,' John said. 'You?'

'Same as ever,' Sam replied, looking through himself in the mirror.

'Take a seat,' Anne said, nodding to the chairs against the wall. Five of the chairs were empty, but one of them had a handful of magazines and newspapers that Anne had arranged in a small display for people to browse whilst they waited.

John sat down and picked up a paper. He looked at the date on top of the page and compared it to the date on his watch. It was today's paper. He took it for granted now, but he remembered his time on St. Budoc's Island, his home island, west of the Hebrides, where they would only get a paper delivery once a week. If you didn't get to the shop quick enough, you'd end up with the previous week's paper and still pay full price for it.

John thought about St. Budoc's every day. It was the reason he was here and the reason he'd probably never leave.

'Are you doing art therapy later?' John asked Sam.

Sam shrugged. His knee was shaking up and down beneath the black barber cape Anne had wrapped over him.

'Oh, try not to move,' Anne said.

'Sorry,' Sam muttered. His knee stopped shaking but John saw the toe of his slipper vibrate as he wiggled his toes instead.

'What's art therapy?' Anne asked. 'That sounds fun.'

Sam didn't answer, so John answered for him. 'You ever take an art class at school? With the poster paints and PVA glue?'

'Yeah,' Anne said. 'We used to spread that glue on our arms so we could peel it off when it dried.'

John laughed. 'It's like that. It's just another form of therapy, but it's nice being creative,' John said. 'I'm no artist, but Sam's really talented. He can paint a mean portrait, can't you, Sam?'

'Is that so?' Anne asked.

Sam shrugged again.

'Oops! Sorry, no moving,' Anne said, trying to be polite.

'Sorry,' Sam said.

'What do you like to paint?' Anne asked.

'I don't really,' Sam said. 'I just do it because they expect us to.'

Anne laid down her golden scissors and picked up a cleaning brush. She'd just finished cutting Sam's fringe and brushed away some of his hair from his forehead, nose, and shoulders. Most of it fell to the floor in clumps but a few of the finer, smaller hairs floated into the room.

Anne sneezed. It startled John and Sam causing them both to jerk in their seats. John chuckled. The sneeze was loud and high pitched and Anne had managed to catch it in the corner of her elbow before it was too late. The nurses in the hospital called the move *The Vampire Sneeze*, which John found funny, because it was reminiscent of the way vampires in old movies held their capes.

'You caught me off guard,' John said.

'Sorry about that,' Anne said. She laid her brush down next to her scissors and plucked a tissue from a box in the corner of the room. She tried to wipe her elbow without either of them seeing, and then plucked a clean tissue from the box.

Sam looked over at the golden scissors lying next to the sink and his hands started to shake. The mallard engraved on the blade glistened in the light. He then locked eyes with John through the mirror. Cut hair, which Anne's brush had missed, was clinging to the sweat breaking out across his forehead.

'You're looking sharp,' John said. He shot him a smile. Sam didn't smile back.

Anne blew her nose and Sam twitched at the second sudden sound. He looked over to her, wiping snot from her nose, then to John in the mirror, and then down at the scissors.

'Sam,' John said, realising that something was off, 'are you feeling alri—'

Sam snatched the golden scissors from the worktop and before John or Anne realised what he was doing, Sam plunged the scissors into the side of his neck with a tremendous blow and then snapped them back out. Blood spurted out of his neck. A spray of blood splattered across the mirror as the scissors fell from Sam's hand and clanked against the floor.

'Sam!' John yelled. He leapt from his seat, grabbed a white towel from the worktop and pressed it against Sam's neck. The blood seeped through the towel and onto the palm of John's hand.

Anne caught sight of the blood and screamed as Sam convulsed. His arms shook wildly. The blood streamed down his neck, under the towel, and over the cape. Some of it pooled in the fabric whilst most of it was flung off.

John turned to Anne. 'Get a nurse,' he said.

Anne backed up against the wall. Her hand covered her mouth. She was too shocked to scream. She just stared at them. Blood was pouring out of Sam's neck and down John's arm. It felt thick and warm.

'Look at me, Sam,' John said. 'Sam, look at me!'

Sam couldn't focus his eyes. They swam around their sockets, as though he'd been drugged. They drifted apart as he relaxed and then shut them.

'Come on Sam, keep your eyes on me.' He grabbed Sam's face with his free hand and straightened it, trying to get Sam to focus on him. Sam opened his eyes a fraction, struggling to stay conscious, before letting them close again.

The towel became too wet to hold in place. He threw it to the floor, grabbed a clean one, and pressed it to Sam's neck. In seconds the towel had turned red. Sam had stopped shaking but was struggling to catch his breath.

John looked in the mirror and realised that Anne was still there, with her back against the wall, staring blankly at John through the mirror.

'Get a nurse!' he yelled.

Anne finally snapped out of her daze. She ran out of the room and down the corridor. Her feet pounded the hard floor and echoed along the hallway.

'Help!' she screamed. 'Help! Nurse! Help!'

THREE

Recall the past so it shan't be forgotten.
An old Hebridean proverb.

Anne Jackson sat on a bench outside of the hospital, facing the beautifully manicured gardens. Rectangles of carefully selected and well looked after flowers added bright colours to the garden, whilst patches of unkempt wildflowers blossomed around tall oaks, elms and maples that dotted the grounds.

She discarded the butt of her cigarette into a bin next to her and immediately lit another one. She tucked the packet back into her purse, knowing full well that she'd be pulling it out again a few minutes later. As she looked over the gardens, she noticed a wild-looking pond a few hundred metres away from her. Swimming on top were several ducks. She shut her eyes, remembering her engraved scissors, and then forced them wide open again. The darkness of her closed eyes was no longer a safe place for her to be. The police had taken her scissors along with her address and said they would return them. Anne wasn't sure if she even wanted them back. She couldn't bear the thought of using those scissors on another client.

It had been several hours since the ambulance had come, and about an hour since she had spoken with the police. She had told the nurses that she needed some time to calm down before she felt steady enough to drive home.

John Calvary spotted Anne out of the window. He had showered and changed into a clean set of clothes. He'd asked the nurses for any news but no one had updated him, so for all he knew Sam Locke was dead. He hoped that he wasn't. He had tried to sleep but couldn't. Nor could he eat, despite feeling so hungry he could vomit.

He went to the cafeteria and ordered two cups of tea. He loaded them onto a tray with two packets of shortbread, and carefully carried it out to the garden. He walked slowly so that he wouldn't spill the tea.

Anne had lit yet another cigarette. She blew smoke from her mouth. It hovered around her like a cloud before being carried away by the breeze.

'I thought you might like a cup of tea,' John said as he stood beside her.

Anne jumped, then said, 'Sorry, I didn't hear you.'

'Mind if I sit with you?' John asked.

'Please,' she said and gestured next to her.

John put the tray down on the glass-topped table and handed her a cup of tea.

'Maybe later,' Anne said. 'I don't think I have the stomach for anything right now.'

'Except a cigarette,' John said.

'Except a cigarette,' Anne muttered back. She handed the pack to John and said, 'Would you like one?'

'No thanks,' John said. 'I'm not sure I want a cup of tea either. I just wanted to see you.' They sat in silence for a few minutes, listening to the sounds of nature. Faint quacks rose from the pond. Distant trees creaked as they swayed, rustling their leaves.

'Have you heard anything?' Anne asked.

'Nothing yet,' John said, 'but I'll keep asking.'

'Do you think he'll be okay?' Anne asked.

'I hope so,' John said. He didn't know what else to say so he just repeated himself. 'I hope so.'

'You acted so quickly,' Anne said, turning to him. 'I just froze. I didn't know what to do.'

'I used to be a professor,' John said. 'The university gave us first aid training every year. I've done it so many times that it's just become second nature to me now. Not that I've ever needed to use it before.'

'I've taken at least two first aid classes,' Anne said, 'but I still froze. He'd be dead if it weren't for you.'

He might be dead anyway, John thought and shook the thought away from him. He struggled to sleep as it was, he didn't need anything else to keep him awake.

Anne looked around them and realised that it was just the two of them. Behind her, through the windows, she saw patients and staff in the sitting room that overlooked the grounds going about their lives, as though nothing had even happened. Maybe the other patients hadn't been told.

'Are you allowed to be outside by yourself?' she asked. 'Should there be a nurse or chaperone or someone with you?'

'It's okay,' John said. 'I'm here voluntarily.'

'You mean you *want* to be here?' Anne asked, frowning.

'No one *wants* to be here. But being here helps.'

'Why *are* you here?' Anne asked and then immediately regretted it. 'I'm sorry. I shouldn't have asked that. That's so rude of me.' She buried her head in her hands.

John laughed. 'It's okay. Don't worry. Everyone wonders the same thing but you're the only one who's been brave enough to ask.'

'It's just that... you seem normal,' Anne said as she lifted her head.

'Normal?' John asked, chuckling.

'Crap. Sorry,' Anne said. 'I didn't mean that.'

'It's fine. I know what you mean,' John said as he tried to reassure her. 'When you think of psychiatric hospitals people think of Bedlam or the insane asylums that killers escape from in the movies. Truth is, for the most part, they're rather normal. At least this one is.'

'This one is more like a castle,' Anne said, looking over her shoulder at the looming building. This side of the hospital only had two turrets, one at each corner. The St. Andrews Cross gently fluttered in the breeze atop a flagpole on the eastern turret.

'It's nice, isn't it,' John said. 'I believe it used to be a convent.'

'A convent?' Anne asked. 'Like witches?'

'No,' John said and laughed. 'A *convent*. Like nuns. They would come here to meditate and pray,' John said, 'and do whatever else it is that nuns do.'

'Oh,' Anne said and hoped her laughter would hide her embarrassment. 'Well, it's a peaceful place to meditate. Is that why you choose to stay here?'

'If I told you why I'm here, I don't think you'd believe me,' John said.

'I'm a hairdresser,' Anne said. 'I hear a lot of unbelievable stories. There's something about sitting in my chair that makes my clients feel like they can tell me anything. You don't have to tell me, but you can trust me if you do.'

John examined her tired face. She wasn't old, maybe in her twenties, but she already had crow's feet around her eyes, which had probably been caused by smoking. Did he really want to tell her his story? Would she just think it was another tall tale from one of her clients? Although he wasn't technically her client... she hadn't actually gotten around to cutting his hair because Sam had— John cut the thought short.

He looked around them to make sure that they were truly alone and that no one else was listening. John trusted her, or at least he believed that he *could* trust her. He leaned towards her and lowered his voice, so that they wouldn't be overheard.

'I saw something,' he said. 'Something that haunts my dreams. Something that I've spent my entire life trying to forget.'

Anne leaned in closer. She furrowed her brow, intrigued. 'What did you see?' she whispered.

'I saw the face of God,' John said. 'Or at least, I saw the face of something that was pretending to be God.'

FOUR

The first sign shall be the fish.
From an ancient Hebridean prophecy.

Many years earlier.

Claire Burns was wrapped up warm for her morning run. She wore thermal leggings, a long sleeve top, and gloves. She had started almost every day with a run, ever since she had left school when she was eighteen. She was in her forties now and had only missed a handful of runs in her life. West Beach was her favourite spot. There was something beautifully eerie about St. Budoc's beaches in the early morning that she had always loved. The waves softly broke against the shore as the mist crept in from the sea and stroked the sand beneath her feet as she ran in the diffused silver of predawn twilight.

As she ran, she noticed something on the sand coming up ahead of her. A dead fish. It must have washed up during the night. The gulls will get it soon. She could smell the brininess of the sea. It was like the fragrance of a fresh oyster.

Claire ran around the fish, careful not to step on it. She looked at it as she ran past. Its skin was dull, as though it had been dead for a little while. As she looked at the fish, she trod on something wet and slipped. She put her arms out for protection as she fell sideways into the sand. She hit the wet sand with a thump.

She looked behind her to see what she had slipped on. It was another dead fish, much larger than the first. She looked around her and realised that she was surrounded by dead fish. Now that she was inside the mist, she could see that the whole beach was littered with hundreds of them, in all shapes and sizes, with some she recognised and some she didn't.

Claire muttered to herself in disbelief as she stood back up.

She started to walk. The density of fish that had washed up on the beach made it impossible for her to continue her jog, but she was now so curious that she didn't want to turn around. She carefully stepped over each one, looking around in shock. The smell of oysters became stronger. It wasn't terribly unpleasant at the moment, but she knew that once the sun had completely risen the smell would become repulsive.

As Claire walked along the beach, and the sheer quantity of fish became apparent, she realised that her initial estimation of there being hundreds of fish was wrong. There weren't hundreds of fish; there were thousands. Some were frightfully large. She couldn't recognise the species, but she passed one that was twice the size of her leg, maybe longer. There were some squid-like creatures, crabs, something that looked like an eel... She even thought that she spotted a tiny little goldfish. The amount and variety of fish was staggering and confusing.

What had happened? Why had they all died? Why had they washed ashore here?

As she continued to walk, she saw something emerge from the mist in front of her. At first, she assumed that it was a boat, but quickly realised that it was something she had never seen before. Something huge. Her heart pounded inside her chest as she stopped in terror.

She tilted her head up in horrific awe of the creature that lay dead before her.

FIVE

There's no stronger connection than family.
From an ancient Hebridean proverb.

The murky green waters surrounded John Calvary and his twelve students. They were kitted out in wetsuits and SCUBA gear. John usually found a strange comfort in being underwater. The pressure of the water felt like he was being coddled in a weighted blanket. The wetsuit, along with its hood and gloves, kept him warm and made him feel safe. Today, however, John was with his students and even though they all had their open water diving certificates, John still had to be on guard. They were his responsibility if anything went wrong.

Lecturing at the university was one thing, he only had to think about his notes and answer his students' questions, but taking his students diving was a completely different kettle of fish. He had to keep his eye on all of them and be able to spot the first signs of disaster. He liked being underwater, sure, but he could do without the added stress.

Ellie Gotlieb lifted her underwater camera to her eye and snapped a photo. A colossal basking shark swam before her, moving gracefully with its mouth wide open. Ellie lowered her camera and floated effortlessly in the water as she watched the shark drift by.

As part of his third-year classes, John took his marine biology students to see basking sharks off of Balmedie Beach, in Aberdeen. The shark was about six metres in length and about ten metres away from them. As it swam, John could see the large white gill rakers that lined its mouth, like thick white support arches designed to stop its mouth from buckling under its own weight. The shark used the gill rakers to strain food from the water. John could see its small, hooked teeth as well. Compared to a great white shark, their teeth seemed harmless. It was a fascinating creature. It was huge, but gentle and only ate the smallest creatures the sea had to offer. The sun refracted off the surface of the water and sent lines of light dancing across the shark's back.

John took a photograph with his own digital camera. Some of his other students had taken GoPros with them for the dive, but John preferred the simplicity of taking a photo.

'It was beautiful,' Ellie said as she climbed up the ladder of the boat. Water fell from her wetsuit, back into the sea. John gave her his hand and helped her up onto the boat. His students were bubbling with excitement as they chatted about the dive.

The sea brings people together, John thought.

'No matter how many times I've seen them, they never cease to amaze me,' John said to Ellie. 'Did you get any good photos?'

'I hope so,' she said. 'You?'

'I'll have to check,' John said. He would download them from his camera when he got back to his hotel room that night. His lips felt dry from the salt water. He dug into his bag, pulled out a strawberry ChapStick and applied it to his lips. He wouldn't normally go for such a fruity flavour, but it was all they sold at newsagents next to the hotel. He then slipped into the cramped toilet on the boat and changed out of his wetsuit. His students felt comfortable just changing on the deck in front of each other, but John wasn't comfortable changing in front of his students.

When the boat docked at the harbour, John and his students walked off the ramp onto the pier, each carrying their own SCUBA gear and eagerly talking to each other. They sounded like kids getting off a rollercoaster. Boats were docked around them, and seagulls squawked as they flew overhead. At the end of the pier, John's assistant Katie Froud was waiting for them. She was dressed in jeans and a t-shirt, which was a lot more casual than what she'd wear to work at the university.

'Here, let me take that,' Katie said as she took the wetsuit from him, leaving him to carry the much heavier oxygen tank.

'Thanks,' John said.

'I got a call from the university,' Katie said. 'Someone's been trying to track you down.'

'Did they say who it was?' John asked.

'No,' Katie replied. 'They didn't want to leave their number either. They said they'll phone your hotel later.'

'Did the university give them my hotel's number?' John asked.

'I guess so,' Katie said.

Who's trying to track me down? John thought. He couldn't think of anyone who didn't already know where to find him.

The hotel he was staying at with his students was a reasonably priced three-star hotel that the university had a deal with. He had stayed there enough times to get to know some of the staff over the years. The students were in the bar downstairs drinking, whilst John was sat on his bed trying to watch the news on a fuzzy television set.

The room's décor lacked inspiration. It was a dark cream colour, with paintings that were glued to the walls. It looked like it hadn't been updated for twenty or thirty years and probably wouldn't be updated for another twenty or thirty years.

John opened the mini-bar and took out a chilled Kit-Kat and a Coke. He didn't think chocolate and Coke went well together, but he was still hungry after dinner and fancied something sweet. He liked to eat Kit-Kats by biting off all the chocolate first, so he could taste the chocolate without the wafer, and then he'd eat the wafer on its own, usually with a mug of Earl Grey.

As he sat there, methodically biting the chocolate off his Kit-Kat, the phone beside his bed rang. The little domed light flashed red with the incoming call.

He picked up the remote, muted the TV, and washed the chocolate down with a mouthful of Coke before answering the phone.

'Hello?' he said.

'Professor Calvary?' someone asked. He recognised her as the Spanish receptionist who had checked him in. She hadn't been here the last time John had stayed at the hotel. He thought her name was Inés but he wasn't certain enough to actually say it out loud.

'Speaking,' John said.

'We have a call for you. Would you like us to connect you?' she asked.

'Who is it?' John asked.

'They didn't say, would you like me to ask?' the receptionist said.

'No, no, it's alright. You can just connect them,' John said and took another sip of Coke.

'One moment please,' the receptionist said.

There was a click and then the phone line screamed with static. It sounded like a microphone had been pointed too close to a speaker. John yanked the phone away from his ear and winced. It was sharp and painful, like when he had his ears syringed. The static abruptly faded away, leaving behind a ringing in his ears and the faint voice of a woman on the other end.

'Hello?' she asked. She sounded distant, as though the phone was in the room next door and John was hearing her through the wall.

John put the phone back to his ear.

'Hello?' she asked again. 'John?'

'Speaking…' John said.

Who is it? he thought. *Who has been trying to track me down?*

'John,' the woman said. 'It's me…'

John sat up. There was a flutter of familiarity in her voice. He thought he recognised her tone, maybe. He couldn't place her though. Was she one of his students perhaps? Or was she—

'It's Sarah.'

Suddenly John was struck by a series of painful, rapid memoires that flashed by in quick succession before he even realised what was happening.

He remembered Sarah, peering into John's room through the crack in his bedroom door. Her eyes were open in shock, and hot panic flooded John's veins.

Then he remembered a stone temple upon a hill by the sea. He could see it clearly in his mind but had no recollection of where it was.

Finally, he remembered the face of a handsome teenager, screaming into a pool of shallow water as bubbles erupted from his half-submerged mouth.

In the second it took Sarah to say her name she had unlocked memories within John that he had spent decades trying to hide away. He sat on the edge of his bed and raised the phone back up to his ear. His hands shook.

'Are you okay?' Sarah asked.

'I- I- I,' John stammered. He swallowed and then said, 'I wasn't expecting to hear your voice. How long has it been?'

'We haven't spoken since Mum and Dad died, have we?' Sarah said.

'Are you still living on St. Budoc's?' John asked, feeling dazed. Just saying the name left a bitter taste in his mouth.

'John, I need you to come back,' Sarah said.

Unthinkable.

'I can't,' John said. *I won't.*

'Something's happening here that I don't understand,' Sarah said.

'I'm sorry,' John said. 'I can't go back.'

After a moment, she asked, 'Are you still teaching marine biology?'

She's trying to change the subject.

'I'm on a trip with my students at the moment,' he told her. 'We're in Aberdeen.'

'There's something you need to see here,' Sarah told him. Her voice quivered a little as she spoke. She must have been trembling on the other end of the line.

Is she afraid, John thought, *or just shocked to speak to me?*

'I can't help you, Sarah,' John said. 'Nothing could make me go back there.'

'Something washed ashore,' Sarah said. 'Something big.'

'A whale?' John asked.

'No one's seen anything like it before,' she said. 'I'm scared.'

John shut his eyes for a moment, trying to understand what she was saying. He pressed his thumb and forefinger into his eyes. Strange shapes and colours swirled before him, like the northern lights or the auras before a migraine. It had been years since he'd heard his sister's voice, and even longer since he had run away from St. Budoc's Island.

'This is all too much, right now,' John said. 'Can we talk about it tomorrow?' He pulled his fingers away and opened his eyes. He'd pressed too hard and his vision was now blurry.

'You didn't come back when Mum and Dad died,' Sarah said softly. John knew she was still hurt by that. 'But you'll want to come back for this. I think it's a new species. I don't know for sure, but you would be able to tell in a heartbeat, wouldn't you?'

'I'm not welcome there. No one wants me to go back,' John said. 'Especially me.'

'You have to,' Sarah said. John could feel the urgent, pleading in her voice. It tugged at him. 'I don't know what's going to happen. It's not just the creature, it's – I need you to come back.' Her voice quivered as she tried not to panic.

He let out a slow, heavy sigh and shut his eyes again. He couldn't go back, could he? Nothing could make him want to return to St. Budoc's. Except maybe Sarah. He missed her greatly but never had the courage to call her himself. It was just too painful. *No,* he finally decided. *I'm never going back.* But there was something about her tone that worried him.

'I can be there next Monday,' John said, not quite believing the words he was saying. Monday felt like it was way too soon to go back to the island. A decade from now felt like it would be too soon. He'd need to speak with Daphne, his therapist, so she could help him to mentally prepare for the trip and come up with some meditative exercises to help him cope with his anxiety whilst he was there.

'Monday's too long away,' Sarah said. 'Can you get here tomorrow?'

John looked at his watch and sighed again. It was getting late. Today was the last day of the trip and he'd need to speak to Katie to make sure that she was okay to take the students back to the university by herself.

'If I get the first train tomorrow morning, I can be there by tomorrow evening,' he said.

So much for mentally preparing.

'Thank you,' Sarah said. She sounded relieved.

John didn't sleep well that night. Maybe it was the sugar in the chocolate and the caffeine in the Coke, or maybe it was the fear of finally returning to St. Budoc's Island.

The train was packed as it left Aberdeen Station. John moved his weekend bag from the seat next to him onto his lap to let someone sit down beside him. His larger case, the one that contained his SCUBA gear, was tucked away with other bags in the luggage holder at the end of the carriage. As people crowded onto the train - mainly morning commuters - they stood up next to each other, holding onto the handrails. They glared down at John both in envy that he had a seat and anger that he was taking up so much space. John tried to avoid eye contact with anyone on the train and when he inadvertently locked eyes with someone, he just smiled an apology and looked away.

John leant his head against the window and watched a young, red-faced man in a blue suit run for the train as it pulled away from the platform. As soon as the man saw the train leave, he threw his briefcase to the floor and swore. His briefcase broke open and papers blew all along the platform and onto the tracks.

Despite the rising anxiety creeping up from his stomach, the soothing rhythms of the train gradually lulled John to sleep. When he opened his eyes again the sun was noticeably higher in the sky. He looked out of the window. They were far from the city now and were travelling through the beautiful Scottish countryside. The hills were dotted with little white sheep grazing on the long grass.

John yawned, covered his mouth with his hand, and looked around him. The train was much quieter now. He put his weekend bag back on the seat next to him and immediately felt relief. He stretched out his legs and tried to relax.

A man pushing a cart walked down the aisle, selling food and drinks. John bought a cup of Earl Grey tea and a tuna sandwich and ate it whilst watching the country shoot by in a green blur.

He could hardly believe that by the evening he'd be back on St. Budoc's Island.

John woke up again, unaware that he had even fallen back asleep. He had a quarter of his sandwich remaining, which he was holding in his lap. Crumbs were scattered over his trouser legs and on the floor. He must have fallen asleep whilst eating.

Through the speakers the train driver made an announcement.

'We're now approaching Mallaig, where this train terminates. All change please. All change,' the driver said.

The train slowly pulled into the small, stone-built station of Mallaig, on the west-coast of Scotland. The station looked like it was at least a hundred years old.

John looked around him. The train was completely deserted now.

Did they really come all this way just for me? he thought.

He scoffed the last part of his sandwich before grabbing his bags. He threw his weekend bag over his shoulder as he wheeled his SCUBA case behind him. As he stepped off the train there was no one else on the platform. They really had come all this way with him as the only passenger. From the front, the station almost looked like a pub, with a large white bay window next to the dark entryway. Next to it he saw a sign for the harbour and followed it. It was only a hundred metres or so from the station.

Mallaig harbour was packed with boats, mainly fishing and sailing boats but there were a few larger boats there too, which were used for cargo and fuel shipping. Rows of white painted houses perched on the tall green hills behind him and there was the familiar sound of seagulls above him.

He found a little ticket office that had a painted sign outside saying it sold tickets for ferries and day trips. He started to wheel his luggage inside, saw how small it was and decided to leave his bags on a bench outside. The décor inside was haggard. There was a faded sign asking for support for the lifeboats and an old brown map pinned to the wall. The clerk was in her fifties, looked utterly miserable, and was so overweight John thought she must have struggled to get into her chair.

'Can I have a single ticket to St. Budoc's please?' John asked.

'You're going to be waiting a while,' the clerk said in a slow, gravelly voice, which had been decayed from years of smoking and drinking.

'How long?' John asked.

'Three days,' the clerk said. 'We have two ferries a week. You just missed the one this morning by, oh let's see...' she checked a paper pamphlet in front of her and then looked at her watch, '...eight hours.'

'I thought they were daily,' John said.

'They haven't been daily for twenty years,' she said and then tried to shift in her chair. The metal legs screeched against the floor.

'Are there any other boats that go to St. Budoc's?' John asked.

'We're the only passenger ferry that travels that far. There's a cargo ship, if you can call it a ship, that goes out once a week, but you'd most likely have to sit on a crate of beans.'

That was the same ship that took out the newspapers, John remembered. All of the island's supplies were delivered once a week on the back of a small boat.

'Great,' John said. 'When does that leave?'

'Yesterday,' the clerk said without a hint of irony.

Behind her, John saw a framed certificate nailed to the wall that said, 'Mallaig Cheerful Service Person of The Year Award – Nominee' And beneath it was her name: Gladys Gath.

Gladys Gath, John thought. *Never has a name so perfectly fit a person.*

John pointed to the certificate and asked, 'Was that recent?' He walked away before Gladys could shout at him.

Not too far from the harbour was an old pub called The Hope and Anchor. John struggled to open the door whilst also managing his luggage. The wheels of his SCUBA case kept catching on the little step, preventing him from dragging it across the threshold. He gave the door a heavy push and it shot open and slammed into the wall so hard that the glass rattled. For a second John thought that he'd broken it.

Everyone inside turned to look at him. There were a handful of patrons. Most of them looked like locals who probably worked on the boats, or in the harbour. There weren't any tourists. Not in this pub.

The landlord stood behind the bar watching him. He had a thick knitted jumper on and a bushy, grey moustache that covered his mouth. He kept his beady eyes on John, watching him struggle to pull his bags through the door, and then watched him drag them across the pub to the bar. He didn't say anything or acknowledge him until he was about a foot away from him.

'Can I get you a drink?' the landlord asked.

'I'm trying to find someone to take me out to St. Budoc's Island,' John said.

'You want the ticket office,' he said, pointing out the door. 'If you go down—'

'I've been there,' John interrupted. He considered making a joke about the clerk who worked there but thought better of it. *They probably all know each other*, he thought. *She might even be his wife*. 'There isn't a ferry for three days.'

'Then I can't help you,' the landlord said.

'Do you know anyone in here who might be willing to take me?' John asked.

'Not off the top of my head. But why don't you have a drink and I'll see if I can think of anyone.'

John took the hint.

'Fine,' John said, 'I'll have a Talisker.'

'We're out of Talisker,' the landlord said.

'I'll have a Laphroaig, then,' John said.

'We're out of Laphroaig too,' the landlord said.

'Well, why don't you tell me what you have and I'll have one of them,' John said.

'No need for sarcasm,' the landlord said, 'especially as I'm the one trying to help you.'

Are you trying to help me? John thought of saying but instead just said, 'Sorry. Just pour me your cheapest whisky.'

'Oh, I don't think I'll be able to find someone to take you for my *cheapest* whisky,' the landlord said.

'Just give me whatever whisky it'll take,' John said.

The landlord reached below the bar and filled a dirty glass with a scant pour of pale whisky.

'Here you go,' he said as he passed it to John.

John handed him a twenty-pound note and waited to see what little change he'd get. The landlord opened the till, dropped in the twenty, and shut it again.

Brilliant, John thought. 'Do you remember anyone now?' he asked.

'Callum!' the landlord shouted across the bar, making John jump.

Callum, a short man in his thirties with a face weathered beyond its years and a beard that hid his neck, turned around. 'Aye?' he said.

The landlord gestured for him to come over. Callum stood up and walked over to them. He walked with a slight limp. John looked down at his feet and saw that the sole of one of his shoes was significantly thicker than the other.

'This gentleman is looking to charter a boat,' the landlord said.

'Oh, aye?' Callum said and shook John's hand.

'Callum has a fishing boat, he might be able to help you out,' the landlord said.

'Aye, I might,' Callum said. 'Where do you want to go?'

'Saint Budoc's,' John said.

Callum shook his head. 'I'm not sure I know that one,' he said.

John turned to the landlord and asked him if he had a map. The landlord pointed over to a framed map on the wall. Callum and John walked over to it. John tapped his finger on St. Budoc's Island, a little island about twenty miles west of the main Hebrides cluster.

'It's a wee one,' Callum said.

'Last time I checked it had a population of about three hundred,' John told him.

'I'll have to navigate us around this one,' Callum said as he tapped a second, smaller island on the map. He read the name, 'St. Machar... I haven't heard of that one either.'

'Actually, that one doesn't exist,' John said.

'It's on the map, isn't it?'

'It only exists on paper,' John told him. 'It was invented by the mapmakers to protect their copyright. If they saw the island on another map, they knew someone had copied them.'

'Oh, that's clever,' Callum said. 'You sure it's not there?'

'If you take me to St. Budoc's you can see for yourself,' John said, looking hopeful.

Callum thought about it for a second and then said, 'Why not? I don't have anything else on. I'll do it for a hundred.'

'How about sixty?' John asked.

'Call it eighty and you've got yourself a boat,' Callum said.

'Deal!' John said and held his hand out. Callum shook it. His hands were rough, warm, and uncomfortably moist. As Callum turned away, John wiped his hand on the back of his trousers.

'Peter,' Callum said to the landlord, 'pour me a whisky for the road.'

The landlord poured him a generous glass of whisky from the top shelf, more generous than what he'd poured for John. It was a rich amber colour. Callum shot it down instantly.

'That'll be one fifty,' the landlord said.

'One fifty?' John asked, shocked. 'That's a lot less than what you charged me.'

'Yeah,' the landlord said, dry as salt, 'but Callum doesn't need a boat.'

SIX

The sea blesses those who bless the sea.
An ancient Hebridean proverb.

With the exception of a few waves, the sea was relatively calm. Callum's fishing boat was able to make good progress as he took John towards St. Budoc's. Not long after they left the harbour, they saw a pod of six white-sided dolphins dancing in and out of the boat's wake. They followed the boat for a few minutes as John watched them in awe. He loved the Scottish dolphins, they seemed so free. They could have been swimming in warmer waters, like the Caribbean or California, but instead they decided to swim here, in the Hebrides. They soon disappeared beneath the waves to continue their frolicking in the hidden depths of the ocean.

After about four hours, John said, 'This is where St. Machar's Island would have been if it existed.' They were both sat in the cockpit with Callum at the wheel and John in the seat beside him. The window next to Callum was open a couple of inches and the fresh sea air filled the cabin.

Callum looked out at the water. 'It's dark here,' he said. 'I've never seen water so dark.'

The water was almost black, like a deep, rich wine. They could make out a soft black outline as though they were floating over an unfathomable abyss, where an island once sat. John had never been near to an abyss, but he imagined that this was what it would be like to stare down into it. Endless.

A little while later, Callum pointed to land ahead of them and asked, 'St. Budoc's?'

John looked out of the window. There she was. She was unmistakable. Her craggy hills jutted out of the water and her green fields, which had always been farmland, adorned them. St. Budoc's Island stood out of the water like a crown.

John felt his stomach sink. He hadn't been back since he had runaway when he was sixteen years old. An uneasy feeling crept over him like a lengthening shadow. *I shouldn't have come back.*

Mist began to float over the sea towards them. By the time they reached the harbour the mist had thickened and had hidden the island's hills. John could feel the dampness of the air across his face. He hadn't noticed it whilst he lived on the island, but the air here wasn't just salty. It was sour.

The harbour was a quarter of the size of the harbour at Mallaig. About sixty boats were moored there. They were exclusively fishing boats, and most of them were significantly smaller than Callum's boat. Fish was the primary source of protein for the islanders and the fishermen were the life-force of St. Budoc's. There was at least one fisherman in every family on the island. If they couldn't fish, the people would starve.

Callum steered his boat towards a dock. He slowed it down until it gently bumped against the wood. He told John to stay in the cabin whilst he hopped off the boat and secured it with ropes.

John looked outside at the foot of the hills and trees. Despite his long absence, they remained the same. John had expected that they would have changed over the last thirty years but they seemed to be exactly the same as when he had left. The mist covered all but the lowest parts of the nearest hills. Unfortunately, it was just as he had remembered it. During their occupation, the Vikings had chopped down most of the trees across the Hebrides to prevent the locals from manufacturing boats. Peculiarly, they had left the trees on St. Budoc's untouched. Everyone had their own ideas as to why, but no one would ever know the real reason.

Sarah was stood on the dock watching them come in. Her hair, which she had so carefully brushed before she had left home, was now fluttering uncontrollably in the wind. She wore a long, plain-looking skirt and a thick, green, knitted cardigan.

Callum looked out of the window at the mist that now completely surrounded them and shrouded the island. 'I need to head back right away,' he said. 'The fog is getting too thick. If I stay any longer, I won't make it home for dinner and I didnae tell my wife I was bringing you here.'

No sooner had John stepped off the boat, Callum started to reverse it back out to sea, and within a few minutes Callum and his boat were lost in the mist.

John walked down the pier and Sarah walked towards him with crossed arms. Now that he was closer, John could see the heavy bags under her eyes. She either hadn't been sleeping or was just getting old. She smiled as she approached him and her eyes immediately swelled with tears.

'John...' she said, almost inaudibly. 'John...'

She wrapped her arms around him with a quiet desperation and hugged him as tight as she could. John felt the warmth of his sister for the first time in decades. She was crying, but she wasn't sobbing. John hugged her back. He had all but forgotten the life he had left behind on St. Budoc's, but as he hugged his sister, he realised just how much he had missed her.

They drove away from the harbour in Sarah's old Ford. Her car was small and must have been twenty years old, but it looked in great condition. St. Budoc's wasn't a massive island, so there weren't too many places that you couldn't walk to, but having a car was a nice convenience. John remembered that as a teenager he would walk almost everywhere. It got to the point where his shoes didn't last him very long and his mother had to repair the worn-out crotches of his trousers so many times that it was more convenient just to drive him anywhere that was further than a twenty-minute walk away.

'How was your journey?' Sarah asked.

'Long,' John said. He told her about what little he remembered from the train journey and about how he struggled to find a boat that would bring him to the island. 'It's strange being back.'

'It's been thirty years,' Sarah said.

'Thirty years?' John thought, rubbing his stubble with the palm of his hand. 'Has it been that long?'

Sarah glanced at him and then looked back at the road. 'You're forty-six now, right?' she asked.

'So, you're forty-four?' John asked. She was looking a lot like their mother now.

'That's right,' Sarah said. 'When we last saw each other we were wee little teenagers.'

They drove into the main town centre. It was a short street with maybe two dozen or so old flagstone buildings, including shops, restaurants, hairdressers, a butchers, a fishmongers… everything you'd need to live on a small island.

The buildings looked tired. Paint was peeling away from signs and several of the shops were empty and looked like they'd been empty for years. He remembered one of them being a quaint little cafe that he'd go to after school sometimes if he didn't have too much homework to do. Sometimes he even did his homework there, whilst sipping watery hot chocolate.

John gazed out of the window with a sad, vacant stare.

This was it. He was back.

He watched the buildings disappear into the mist behind him.

'So have you seen the animal that washed ashore?' John asked.

Sarah nodded. 'Aye, but I wish I hadn't.'

The car park at West Beach was overflowing with cars. John didn't know how many cars there were on the island, but he guessed that every one of them must have been crammed into that little car park. Sarah parked on the road leading up to the car park, which was nearer to Tabi's Fish Bar than to the beach. They walked through the car park and to the stairs that led down to the beach.

The stone stairs were wet from the mist, so John tightly gripped the handrail as he descended. It was cold in his fist. He saw the immense number of fish scattered on the sand. Thousands of dead fish, just washed up on the shore.

What caused this? John asked himself. He'd seen mass mortality before, at a salmon farm who had lost half of their stock because of a sudden spike in water pollution, but he'd never seen anything on this scale before.

Once they were on the beach, John could see a crowd of about a hundred people gathered further down the beach, quietly chatting amongst themselves.

They must be gathered around the creature that Sarah saw, John thought.

And then, out of the mist, a looming figure appeared. How could he have been so blind as to not see it until now? Rising over the crowd he could see the dark shape of the creature's back. It sloped up out of the crowd and then disappeared again, like a slick, oily hill.

'What the hell is that thing?' John asked. He became aware of how fast his heart was beating. Sarah glanced at him. His shock seemed to unnerve her.

A strong, fishy odour hovered over the beach, like an overwhelming fish market. John couldn't tell if it was from the creature, the dead fish, or both. It was probably both.

They walked into the group of people. John pushed past several people on either side of him until he made it to the front of the crowd and could clearly see the creature with his own eyes.

He was horrified.

His eyes widened as his mouth fell open, aghast.

Lying dead on the beach in front of him was a gigantic serpentine sea-creature. Its head was over five metres tall. Vicious, serrated teeth overhung its lips like a bastardised anglerfish. It had two huge fish-like eyes, with dark irises and pupils that were black and glossy, and behind them it had four much smaller eyes that trailed off behind, like perfectly-polished black marbles. In total, it had ten eyes.

What horrors have you seen? John thought. Its similarities to some deep-sea creatures made John think that the creature must have lurked in the darkest, deepest parts of the ocean. Were there more creatures like this down there? He shivered.

The creature's skin was covered in light scales with a texture somewhere between octopus skin and snake skin. It looked somewhat like a snake but definitely wasn't any species of serpent John had seen. Its skin was ever so slightly iridescent, like a trout or a python, but with the rubbery texture of an octopus or squid or some other nightmarish cephalopod. The most fitting word that sprang to mind was: *dragon*.

John looked out at the rest of the body, which seemed to stretch endlessly into the sea until it was lost beneath the waves in the mist. It was huge. He couldn't tell exactly how long it was, but there would be time to measure it later. He was awe-struck by the sheer magnitude of the thing. Its head alone was the size of a double-decker bus, in both height and width. The blue whale was considered to be the largest animal of all time, even bigger than the largest plesiosaur ever found. This creature, whatever it might be, appeared to be larger than both combined.

Its brain must be huge! John thought. *A creature of such a size must have intelligence. It must have had abstract thought. It must have...* The last word haunted John: ...*community.*

There couldn't just be the one creature. There had to be more. It was biologically impossible for there to just be the one. Not unless this was the last one of its kind. John shook that thought away. He'd worry about that later. There was so much he didn't know, and normally as a marine biologist he would jump at the chance of getting to study a new species, but upon seeing the creature for the first time he realised that there was so much he didn't *want* to know.

John turned to look at the faces of the quietly horrified crowd behind him. They must have been stood there for hours, just staring at it. Wondering what it might be and what it would mean for their island lives. John saw an older man, a guy in his sixties with a grey beard, who was wearing wellington boots. He was shaken and erratic. He looked in absolute terror at the monstrous carcass in front of him. Whilst everyone else appeared dazed, it seemed like, to him, the creature had significance. Then he locked eyes with John. For a split second they stared at each other.

The man recognised John instantly and, if it was even possible, he looked even more afraid. He turned and ran away. No one seemed to pay him any attention. Seeing as how scared everyone was, someone running away wasn't unexpected. *Who was that?* John thought as he watched him run down the beach and into the mist. There was a familiarity about him. He might have recognised him had it been thirty years earlier.

John looked ahead of him at a pot-bellied, uniformed policeman in his mid-forties. He was talking with Claire Burns. John walked over to them both. Sarah hesitated to follow, preferring the comfort of the crowd, but eventually followed behind him.

'Does anyone know what this is?' John asked the policeman.

Claire looked at the policeman, hoping he'd take control of the situation. He just looked at John in confusion.

'Who are you?' he asked. 'You're not from here...' As a policeman on a small island, he knew everyone, and if he couldn't remember their first names he would at least know their last names. A foreigner stuck out like a wolf in a dog park and were considered by some to be just as dangerous.

'Professor Calvary,' John started to introduce himself. 'I'm from St. Andrew's University—'

Sarah stepped behind John and smiled at Claire. 'Hi Claire.'

'Hi Sarah,' Claire said.

'How the hell did you hear about this?' the policeman asked in total bewilderment.

'When did it appear?' John asked, ignoring his question and stepping towards the creature.

Claire opened her mouth to answer but the policeman cut in before she could speak.

'This is a police matter,' he said. 'I'm going to need you to step away.'

'Did all the fish wash ashore before or after that thing?' John asked, ignoring him.

'What does it matter?' he asked. 'As I said, I need you to step away.'

'Well,' John said, 'if the fish washed ashore before the creature then it means that there's something in the water that caused all of their deaths. If they washed up after it then the fish probably died as a result of the death of...' he gestured to the creature, '...whatever this thing is.'

He stared at John in incredulity then turned to Sarah and said, 'Did you invite him here, Sarah? We said no outsiders…'

'Mitchell,' Sarah said, 'he's my brother.'

Mitchell turned back to John and studied his face in stunned disbelief. 'John Calvary?' Mitchell said. 'Is that really you?'

'Yes?' John said. Was he supposed to recognise him too?

The policeman laughed in relief and then said, 'It's me, Mitchell Miller. We were in Mr. Sutherland's class together!'

As it all came flooding back to John, it was his turn to laugh.

'Mitchell?' John asked with a huge smile on his face. 'I didn't recognise you!'

'How the hell have you been?' Mitchell grabbed hold of John's hand, without giving John a chance to accept or reject the handshake, and shook it vigorously with both hands. 'I never thought you'd come back.' He laughed from his belly with friendly excitement.

'Neither did I,' John said, 'but Sarah phoned me yesterday and…' he gestured to the creature again, '…here I am.'

'Do you remember Claire?' Mitchell asked, turning towards Claire.

'Sarah and I were at school together,' Claire said.

John recognised her. Sarah didn't have many friends as a teenager because there weren't many teenagers on the island to be friends with, but he remembered her frequently hanging out with Claire Burns, recalling them doing their homework together at the kitchen table.

'Claire is the one who found the creature yesterday morning,' Sarah said.

'That must have been a shock,' John said.

'Aye, it was,' Claire said, looking over at the creature and seeming confused as to why she hadn't woken up from her dream yet.

Behind Claire, John watched as two fishermen, one in his sixties and the other in his twenties, looked at the fish lying on the beach. The older of the two fishermen picked up a fish, looked it over and sniffed it. He grimaced at its smell and threw it over his shoulder before picking up the next one. The younger fisherman was doing the exact same thing. Smelling the fish, grimacing, and throwing it over his shoulder behind him. There wasn't a fish they smelled that they didn't throw over their shoulder. John thought he saw the younger fisherman pick up one of the fish discarded by the older fisherman, only to throw it over his own shoulder.

'What are they doing?' John asked.

Mitchell turned around to see what John was referring to. 'Oh, they're checking the fish to see if any can be salvaged, but not only are they all dead, they've all gone off too. Can't eat a single one. What a waste,' he turned back to face John and asked, 'What do you think that means?'

'They must have died before they washed ashore,' John said. 'Maybe they all died a few miles off the coast and washed up here. But you'd expect at least the birds to have gotten to them,' John said as he watched half a dozen gulls sitting on the beach, looking at the wasted fish, 'but not even the gulls want to eat them.'

'You said you're a professor now?' Mitchell asked.

'Yeah, I'm a marine biologist,' John said.

'So you could tell us what this thing is?'

'That's why I called him,' Sarah said. 'If anyone could identify it, it'd be John.'

'Maybe if we pull a team together to look it over, they could—'

'Can you tackle it by yourself?' Mitchell interrupted.

John looked over the creature. Waves were crashing against its body where it sank beneath the surface. He shook his head before saying, 'It's just too big. Let me bring a team over and—'

'I'm sorry, John,' Mitchell said. 'I'm grateful that you came back, really I am, but this is a matter best left for us islanders. It stays on the island. No outsiders. Present company excluded.'

'Most of it is out at sea. It's too dangerous to examine by myself,' John said.

Mitchell looked thoughtful for a second and then said, 'My nephew, Lawrence, could help. He's only eighteen but he can dive. What do you say?'

'I guess I don't have a choice,' John said. 'If he's willing, I'll accept all the help I can get.'

John looked up at the sea monster's head, then along its body. As a scientist, he felt like he should be excited about confronting the unknown, but instead he was terrified. It wasn't just because the creature looked dangerous but because it signalled something so much bigger than itself. It signalled the existence of more unknown and unspeakable horrors.

SEVEN

Adversity turns strangers into friends,
but whisky turns them into family.
An old Hebridean proverb.

Sarah and John pulled up in front of Sarah's house, which used to be their old family home. It was a small stone house that had been built before the wars. It was made of large, local stones that were a mixture of brown, grey and yellow in colour. It had two chimneys, one on either end of the house, and a relatively new roof. Several other houses on this stretch of meandering road had thatched roofs, as they all once had, but most of them had been replaced for the sake of practicality. John recognised it instantly. He would have given anything to feel happy about being home, but this wasn't his home. Not anymore. It hadn't been for a long time.

On either side of the road were grassy banks and large boulders. There were nine houses in total along this part of the road. The road was up a hill, which normally allowed you to see the sea, but the mist was so thick, and the sky was almost completely dark, that John couldn't even see the end of the road.

John unloaded his luggage from the car whilst Sarah unlocked the front door. He felt weird being back. The last time he was there was when he was sixteen, and still lived there with his family.

Inside, the house was in desperate need of decoration. The furniture was old, and most of it was the same furniture that he had grown up with, apart from a new sofa, television, and a curiosity cabinet filled with their old family crockery and the few glasses that had survived the years. Sarah didn't use them anymore but couldn't face throwing them away. The crockery had been a wedding present to their parents from their great-grandparents, so she didn't even feel comfortable selling them or donating them to the charity shop.

John set his bags down in the entryway as he looked around. 'I can't believe you still live here,' he said, amazed at how little had changed.

'I didn't want to sell it,' Sarah said. 'How could I let someone else live here? We grew up here. There are too many memories.'

And a lot of ghosts, John thought as he walked upstairs, looking at the old family photos hanging on the wall. Some of the photos hadn't changed since he left, but Sarah had added several new ones of their parents, who looked much older than John had ever seen them. He looked at a photo of his Mum and Dad taken outside this house. He recognised a lot of Sarah in his Dad, and himself in his Mum. It was a scary glimpse into their futures, albeit with their sexes reversed.

'I never thought I'd be back here,' John said.

'Do you mind sleeping in your old room?' Sarah asked.

'Is there nowhere else?' he asked. He'd rather sleep in a grave than his old room.

'Mum and Dad's room is full of boxes, and I'm sleeping in my room.'

John looked at Sarah and said, 'You still sleep in the same room?'

'It's home,' Sarah said. 'It might not be for everyone, but I'm happy.'

'Why didn't you move into Mum and Dad's room?' John asked.

Sarah shrugged. 'It didn't feel right.'

John couldn't imagine living in this house, let alone sleeping in his old bed every night. He would hate it. He had no idea how Sarah managed it. He thought that maybe she was clinging too hard to the past and to her childhood, or maybe she was too scared to step out into the world by herself and this old house made her feel safe.

Sarah opened the door to John's room for him. The slight breeze from the door lifted a haze of dust that filled the bedroom. The room was lit by a single naked bulb, which cast hard shadows onto the walls.

'I'm still trying to order in the right lampshade,' Sarah said. 'Mrs. McWhinnie's is the only shop that could get one in for me but she's still waiting for a catalogue delivery.'

The walls were bare, apart from the faint ghosts of where his posters used to hang. His parents never repainted his room after he left. A photo hung on the wall, an old school photo of John and Sarah sat together, smiling, when they weren't even teenagers yet. It was the only decoration in the room and John suspected that Sarah put that up as soon as she knew that he was coming.

John put his bags down next to the bed. It was the same one he had slept in as a child, an old bed made of a dark, varnished wood.

He lay down on his back and looked at the familiar shapes on the stucco ceiling. He had spent years staring up at them and the oppressive feeling of the house now made it feel as though they were staring back. He sought out some familiar patterns; a boat, a bird, a fish, and started to remember thoughts and feelings from a lifetime ago. As soon as he had left the island he had forgotten all of these little familiarities that he had lived with, and now they were all coming back to him.

John then became aware of the pain in his ankles. He looked down and saw that his feet were hanging over the edge of the bed. His ankles dug into the hard wooden frame as they stretched over the bottom of the mattress.

At least some things have changed, he thought.

On the way to the pub, Sarah and John stopped off at the newsagents that Sarah owned. It was a small shop, as most of the shops on the high street were. Although it was predominantly a newsagents - selling drinks, confectionary, cigarettes, and alcohol - it also doubled as a quick-stop grocery store. She had a small display of fresh local veg and eggs, and some essential items like tinned goods, dried beans and pastas, and toiletries.

Sarah pushed open the door and a little bell on top of the door jangled. Inside, Beth Rabbit was sat behind the counter reading a paperback copy of Treasure Island with an empty bottle of 7up next to the till. Beth was a teenager, about fourteen or fifteen, John thought, with soft, light curly hair that bounced over her shoulders as she stood up.

'Hi Beth,' Sarah said.

'Hi Sarah,' Beth said as she slipped her bookmark into her book. 'It's been quiet so I thought I'd catch up on my reading for school.'

'Don't worry about it,' Sarah said. 'I get bored when it's quiet too. This is my brother, John.'

John smiled and extended his hand to shake Beth's. She had a green friendship bracelet tied to her wrist. He thought he recognised her from somewhere but couldn't imagine how. He had probably gone to school with one of her parents and recognised some similarities.

'It's nice to meet you,' Beth said. 'Sarah's told me a lot about you.'

'Only good things I hope,' John chuckled.

'Have you moved back here?' Beth asked.

'No, I've just come to look at the creature that washed up on the beach.'

'John's a marine biologist,' Sarah butted in.

'Oh, do you know what it is then?' Beth's face brightened with excitement.

'No idea,' John said.

The girl's face fell in disappointment but she carried on. 'My younger brother, Nathan, believes it's an alien,' she said. 'But he's ten and watches too much TV.'

John laughed. 'We all watch too much TV,' he said. 'What do you think it is?'

Beth pulled her lips into her mouth and looked up at the ceiling as she thought. 'Well, I don't believe in aliens,' she said, 'and it doesn't look a bit like Nessie, so…' she paused, '…maybe it's some unknown deep-sea creature, like those ugly fish with a light above their heads.'

'Anglerfish,' John said.

'Yeah,' Beth said. 'Something ugly like that.'

John chuckled.

Sarah let Beth head home. She packed up her book into her bag and took a carton of apple juice for the walk home. She punched the plastic straw into the little metallic hole and took a sip as she opened the door.

'Do you need me tomorrow?' Beth asked as she hovered in the doorway.

'Just to help with the delivery, and then you can go,' Sarah told her.

John watched her leave and then saw her wave to someone she knew in one of the other shops. She had a happy spring in her step.

'She's sweet,' John said.

'Yeah, she hasn't been working here long,' Sarah said. 'But her mum is sick – she heads to the mainland every couple of weeks for treatment – so I thought it might be helpful for her to have something to do to keep her mind off things.'

'That's really kind of you,' John said. He always knew Sarah had a loving and caring side. She was like that when they were teenagers. It was part of what made it so difficult to leave home, and the only nice part about coming back. It was nice to see her keep her good traits as an adult. It made him proud. 'Who is her mum?' John asked. 'She looks familiar.'

'Briony McPhee,' Sarah said. 'Now Briony Rabbit. She married Tom Rabbit. I think they were a few years above you at school. Do you remember them?'

John shook his head. Maybe he'd recognise them if he saw a picture.

He looked around the shop as Sarah counted the money in the till. Sarah had bought the shop from Mr. and Mrs. Reid when they had retired. Their children had both moved to the mainland and Sarah didn't want to see the shop in the hands of anybody else, so she bought it. Unlike her home, Sarah had kept the shop a little more up to date. The displays looked new, the glass on the drinks fridge was shiny, and it looked like she had replaced the flooring. John swept the floors for something to do whilst Sarah counted the money in the till, locked up the shop, and turned off the lights.

The Mariner's Dog was the island's favourite pub. It was at the end of the high street, only a three-minute walk from Sarah's shop. It didn't have the traditional stone-look as many of the buildings had. Instead, it was a light painted brick, with a soft green trim around the windows. Outside was a painted pub sign of a small white dog, looking alert. Its legs were stiff, and its nose was pointing towards whatever it was looking at. The paint had faded over the years, and some of it had even chipped away. John thought he remembered there being a sailing boat behind the dog, but now there was only the wood that the sign was painted on.

As soon as they entered the pub, John was hit by the smell of beer, whisky, and chips. There was a crackling fireplace with a few small flames licking the burning logs. There were several booths and dark-wood tables, and about twenty people drinking inside.

John felt uncomfortable. A few people had turned to stare at him, but even more were watching him out of the corners of their eyes, hoping their curiosity and animosity would go unnoticed. It made John feel stiff.

'They don't want me here,' John said quietly to Sarah.

'It's been a long time,' Sarah tried to reassure him. 'They probably don't even recognise you.'

The pub had three different beers on tap, and behind the bar was a modest collection of bottles and glasses. The barman was a man named Angus Brown. He wore a cream shirt and was clean-shaven. John recognised him instantly.

'Is that Angus?' John asked.

'Yeah,' Sarah said. 'Claire's dad.'

As John and Sarah approached the bar, Angus smiled at him and said, 'Welcome home, John.' Apart from Sarah, he was the only person who seemed genuinely happy to see him back on the island. Mitchell had seemed to be excited once he had realised who he was, but before then he was cold and unwelcoming.

'You haven't aged a bit,' John said as he shook Angus' hand.

'You have,' Angus said and laughed. His smile revealed a multitude of wrinkles over his face. 'What would you like to drink?'

John turned to Sarah and asked what she'd like.

'Orange juice, please,' she said.

Angus reached behind the bar and pulled out a carton of orange juice. He poured it into a glass, dropped in a single ice cube and passed it to Sarah.

'And you, John?'

'I'll have a whisky please,' John said and wondered if he'd have as much trouble ordering one here as he did in Mallaig.

'We only stock St Budoc's,' Angus said. 'Made by our very own Whisky Master. Isn't that right, Wallace?' He looked over to Wallace Burns, a man in his forties, wearing a tweed-jacket. Wallace turned around and raised his own glass of whisky in acknowledgement.

'Best whisky in the country,' Angus said.

'Aye. Best whisky in the country,' Wallace slurred.

'Well, you'd better pour me a glass,' John told him.

'Good choice,' Angus said.

It's the only choice, John thought.

Wallace raised his glass again and, without turning to look at him, said, 'Best decision you'll ever make.'

Angus poured John a very generous glass of St. Budoc's whisky and passed it to him. All it took was a single sip for his scepticism to dissolve. The whisky was delicious. It smelled of fresh peppermint leaves and lemon peel. He savoured the whisky in his mouth. It was full of honey, and heather, and an ever so subtle, pleasing trail of smoke on the finish.

Wow.

'This is incredible,' John said.

'Best whisky in the country,' Wallace muttered again. It was becoming his catchphrase.

'How much do I owe you?' John asked.

'It's on the house.' Angus smiled.

'Are you sure?' John asked. It was a hell of a lot better than the twenty quid he paid for the glass of piss in Mallaig.

'Welcome home, John,' Angus said. 'It's good to have you back with us.'

Sarah and John sat down at a table along the wall.

'Wallace is Claire's husband,' Sarah told John, keeping her voice low so that Wallace wouldn't hear.

'And Angus is Claire's dad,' John said.

'That's right.'

'Sounds like there's a bit of nepotism going on with Angus' whisky selection.' John took another sip and added, 'Not that I'm complaining. This stuff is delicious. Do you want a sip?'

'No thank you,' Sarah said. 'I stopped drinking after Mum and Dad died.'

They chatted for a few minutes before Mitchell Miller walked into the pub with his nephew Lawrence. Lawrence was eighteen years old. He had dark-blonde hair, and a face so smooth John didn't think that he could even grow a beard yet. They spotted John and Sarah and walked over to them.

'This is my nephew, Lawrence,' Mitchell said. 'He'll be able to help you examine the creature.'

John stood up and shook Lawrence's hand. His eyes were a stormy-blue. John felt like it was looking into the depths of the sea. Lawrence smiled.

John suddenly remembered another boy he knew with the same beautiful smile and realised how sweaty his palms had become. *Patrick.* He hid his momentary shock and quickly said, 'It's nice to meet you,' before it became too uncomfortable.

Neither Mitchell nor Lawrence noticed, but as John glanced at Sarah, she looked him up and down. She could tell that John was feeling a little flustered. John looked away as he felt the warmth of the whisky rush to his cheeks.

'It's nice to meet you too,' Lawrence said, still smiling. He pulled out one of the wooden chairs and sat down opposite John. Mitchell went over to Angus and ordered two pints. One for him and one for Lawrence. He brought them back to the table and sat them down on a couple of beer mats, which advertised a Scottish beer that John had never heard of.

'How's everything on the beach?' John asked.

Mitchell swallowed a mouthful of beer and licked the froth from his lips. 'It's still there,' he said. 'Do you think you'll be able to identify it?'

'The best we can hope to do is categorise it,' John said. 'There's nothing to identify as no one will know what it is. I'll have a look and try to find out what genus, if any, it may belong to, if it's native to these waters, or if it washed in from afar, and what may have killed it.'

Lawrence was nodding along, hanging on to his every word.

'Well, that's a good start,' Mitchell said and took another sip of beer.

'Mitchell said that you can dive?' John asked Lawrence.

'That's right,' Lawrence said. 'I got my PADI Open Water last summer. My friend, Greg, and I went down to Plymouth to surf but ended up taking the PADI course instead.'

'Oh, could Greg help as well?' John asked, looking from Lawrence to Mitchell and then back at Lawrence again until one of them answered.

'He actually lives in Plymouth now. He decided to stay down there. So probably not,' Lawrence said and smiled again.

That smile, John thought as Patrick's face flashed in his mind. *I'll never forget it.*

'A lot of the creature is underwater,' John said, looking down at his whisky. 'We'll need to dive if we want to find out how long it actually is. Will you be okay with that?'

'Absolutely,' Lawrence said, nodding.

'And you have your own gear?' John asked.

'I do.'

'That's great,' John said. 'I don't know many youngsters who have their own SCUBA gear.'

'Well, there's nowhere on the island to rent it from,' Lawrence said. 'It just made sense to buy my own.'

'We should start tomorrow morning,' John continued. 'Early, so we can make the most of the day.'

'Sounds good to me,' Lawrence said.

'John?' someone shouted. 'John Calvary, is that really you?'

John looked around to see who was calling his name. He spotted Ben Walters rushing over to him. Ben was almost six feet tall and, despite not being muscular, he looked strong. He had a little bit of salt-and-pepper stubble. He probably hadn't shaved since yesterday.

'Ben?' John said.

John stood up. Ben grabbed John's hand and shook it with vigorous enthusiasm. His smile stretched from ear-to-ear.

'I heard that you were back. You're here to look at the… to look at what washed ashore, right?' Ben asked. 'You're a marine biologist now?'

'That's right,' John said and thought, News *travels fast on the island.* 'I'm going to try to figure out what it is at least.' He loosened his hand to end the handshake, but Ben didn't let go.

'It's terrifying, that's what it is, isn't it?' Ben said, firmly gripping John's hand. 'And you really want to get up close? I couldn't imagine touching that thing.'

John felt the heat of people staring at him. Despite the smiles of the few people he'd met so far, he had the unshakable feeling that his presence was making everyone uncomfortable.

'Why don't you sit down and join us?' John asked and gestured to the table, hoping that they could sit and talk quietly, averting the gaze of the unhappy patrons.

'Thanks, but I'm okay standing. I'm trying to get my steps in,' Ben said. 'Ten thousand a day, they say, right? How am I supposed to get that on a wee li'l island like this? Say, aren't you worried about parasites or disease? You've seen what it's done to those fish. It could be anything that's caused this.'

'I'll take precautions,' John said. He started to feel like Ben was being too nosey. John wasn't entirely sure how he'd examine the creature yet. He needed to figure out the safest, most efficient way for him and Lawrence to proceed.

Ben quietened his voice and said, 'Well, just be careful.' He narrowed his eyes and nodded his head. After a moment, he finally let go of John's hand.

Is he warning me or threatening me? John wondered. He couldn't tell. Either way he didn't like the way he had said it. John clenched and unclenched his fist by his side. His hand hurt.

Before John could say anything, Ben shouted, 'Hey Angus. Two whiskies!'

'Come get them yourself,' Angus shouted back.

John and Sarah chatted with Mitchell and Lawrence for the rest of the evening. John and Mitchell did most of the talking. They spoke mainly about the creature on West Beach, but John also told them about his work as a professor, and Mitchell spoke about taking over as the Chief Police Officer on the island. Mitchell and Sarah filled him in on some key events that had happened since he had been away - the change in boat schedule, a new monthly newspaper that covered the Outer Hebrides, Alan Stapledon's affair with Barbara Amwell - but really St. Budoc's Island hadn't changed as much as John had expected. Or as much as he had hoped.

Whenever John went on holiday and returned to his home in St. Andrews, he always expected everything to be drastically different - his neighbours had burned down their house, a new restaurant had opened, a massive scandal at the university – but none of that ever happened. It was just that John had felt like *he* should have been changed by his trip, and returning home was proof that life was the same, and his holiday, although fun, wasn't the life-altering soul-searching experience he thought he needed.

As the night went on, and as John drank more and more of St. Budoc's whisky – the stuff really was delicious – he started to feel more at ease and stopped noticing the side-glances the other drinkers were giving him. Spending quality time with Sarah, and meeting some familiar faces, really felt like coming home. Despite that, he'd never forget why he ran away in the first place. The whisky was making him feel more welcome than he was. He couldn't forget that.

John struggled to push open the pub door as they left.

'It's a pull, not a push,' Sarah said.

John corrected himself and pulled the door open instead. He'd had more to drink than he realised.

Unless Wallace's whisky was stronger than others? John thought as he stumbled out of the door.

'It was strange seeing Ben again,' John said. 'I haven't seen him since...' He trailed off, not wanting to finish the sentence.

'Since Patrick died?' Sarah asked.

John wasn't ready to relive those memories.

'Since I left the island,' John said instead.

'My car!' Sarah yelled as they walked into the street.

Sarah and John rushed over to her car to find that the windscreen had been shattered. It looked like someone had hit it with a hammer or had thrown a brick at it. The glass was a spider-web of cracks.

'Who would want to do this to me?' Sarah said as she ran her shaky fingers over the glass. Her eyes filled with tears. John tugged her wrist away.

'Don't do that,' he said. 'You might cut yourself.'

Sarah saw a piece of paper tucked beneath the window wiper, and against the shattered glass. She plucked it from its resting place and unfolded it. She glanced at it and then passed it to John to look at. Scribbled in permanent marker, and in a messy scrawl, were two words:

GO HOME.

Go home? John thought. He felt himself sobering up. He'd let the whisky lull him into a false sense of security. It was wrong of him to come back to the island. The sea creature may be a new specimen, and may be one of the greatest finds of the century, but he was unsafe here. He was unsafe as a teenager, and he was unsafe as an adult. He tried to shake off those feelings when he arrived, but this was proof. He really shouldn't have returned.

They drove home. Sarah leant forward, so she could see out of the uncracked parts of the windscreen. The cracked glass was as dangerous to her driving as her tears were. Every few seconds she'd dab at her eyes with the end of her sleeve and mutter something about why anyone would want to do this. She gripped the wheel so tightly that the tips of her fingers were turning white. If John were even a little bit more sober, he would have insisted on driving, but in his condition his driving would be as unsafe as Sarah's was.

They pulled up to Sarah's house. John got out and opened the door for her.

'Thank you,' she muttered, and dabbed her eyes with her sleeve again.

John heard something rustling nearby. He looked around him, but the mist was still dense. He could only see about twenty feet around him.

'Did you hear that?' John asked.

'Hear what?' Sarah replied.

John saw the dark shape of a man emerge from the bushes. He had been hidden amongst the mist and shadows but now he stepped forward into the dim moonlight.

'Go inside,' John said softly to Sarah.

Sarah quickly unlocked the front door and scampered inside.

The man lurched towards John with drunken determination. It was too dark, too misty, and John was too far away from the man to see his face. *This must be who smashed the windscreen. It has to be.*

'Don't come any closer,' John warned. A rush of adrenaline dispersed more of his drunken state. He felt himself becoming more alert, more aware, and more sober.

The man kept staggering towards him, and as he lurched closer, the diffused moonlight illuminated his haggard face. It was the man he had seen on the beach. John finally recognised him. He was Victor Walters. He had aged a lot since the last time he had seen him. It looked like he had taken up the bottle and hadn't showered in a few days. It broke John's heart to see Patrick's dad like this.

'Victor?' John asked.

'You shouldn't be here,' Victor spat, pointing his finger as he wobbled forward. He swayed as though the floor was quaking beneath him.

'Victor,' John said, 'did you do this?' He gestured to Sarah's windscreen.

'You don't understand,' Victor slurred. 'You have to *leave!*' As he shouted the last word his whole body tensed. His arms became rigid by his sides and spit flew from his mouth.

The front door blasted open and Sarah came rushing over to Victor. In her hand was a large kitchen knife. It was bright. She pointed it towards Victor. Her whole body shook with determination. Her body jerked as she took short, quick steps towards Victor.

Victor's eyes opened wide. He held up his palms in surrender and shuffled backwards.

'Get away from my house!' Sarah shouted. She sounded unhinged. 'If I see you anywhere near me again, I'm going to *gut* you!' Her lips trembled.

John had never seen Sarah so angry before. They had fights as kids, like any siblings do, but seeing her like this, so uncontrollably aggressive as an adult, frightened him. It also frightened Victor. He spun around as quickly as his drunken legs would allow and ran away. He ran down the road unsteadily, before he disappeared into the mist, and the night became still again with nothing but the breeze and the distant lapping of the sea.

Sarah dropped the knife in shock. It clattered against the ground. Her whole body was shaking. John ran over to her and held her tight, but her arm was still pointed out, as though she were still holding the knife. As she sobbed in relief, and as John tightly hugged her, she gradually calmed down and relaxed. Her body became less rigid and her hands found John's back as she eventually hugged him too. She heaved deep sobs into his shoulder.

John led her inside and sat her down on the sofa. He boiled the kettle and made her a mug of tea. He dropped in two teaspoons of sugar and a glug of full-fat milk. He passed it to her and she held it with both hands, letting its warmth comfort her. She smiled up at him. Her eyes were puffy from crying, and tiny little red dots had appeared beneath them.

'Are you alright?' John asked.

Sarah nodded.

'Do you want to talk about it?'

Sarah shook her head before looking down at her feet. 'No thank you,' she muttered. 'Not tonight.'

They sat there in silence until she had finished her tea and then went to bed. As John lay in his childhood bed, staring straight up at the ceiling with his feet hanging over the bottom of the mattress, he heard Sarah gently sobbing through the walls. She was still crying when he had finally fallen asleep.

EIGHT

The waters will reveal their age.
From an ancient Hebridean prophecy.

Lawrence pulled up outside of Sarah's house before sunrise. He drove a small, blue Mini Cooper, which was at least twenty-five years old. It was the perfect car for an island as small as St. Budoc's but wouldn't last a mile on a motorway. John was up early and was already waiting for Lawrence inside. He was sat on the sofa, with his gear in front of him, and a half-finished cup of tea in his hands when he saw the headlights flash through the downstairs window. He gulped down the rest of his tea, placed the cup in the sink, opened the door, and greeted Lawrence with a smile.

'Is all this gear going to fit?' John asked, looking at his SCUBA case. It was a large, black hardcase with SCUBA embossed on the side. He'd managed to bring it all the way across the country on the train and a fishing boat, but Lawrence's Mini was much smaller than either of those.

'Just put it on the back seat,' Lawrence said. He got out and helped him load the case onto the back seat, next to his own equipment. It was a tight fit and by the time they got everything packed in, John wondered if Lawrence would even be able to see as he drove.

As they got into the front of the car, Lawrence noticed Sarah's cracked windscreen. 'What happened to the car?' he asked.

'I'll tell you about it on the way,' John said. 'Will you be able to see with all the stuff in the back?'

Lawrence looked into the rear-view mirror, and then over his shoulder. 'I guess not,' he said.

'Should we rearrange it?' John asked.

'Nah,' Lawrence said dismissively. 'Let's live dangerously.' He cracked John a smile and laughed as he turned the car around.

As they drove towards West Beach they drove through patches of mist in the soft, silver light. The island was eerily peaceful. A flock of sparrows landed in a tree together, preparing to sing their morning songs, and John thought he saw a bat, flying home to roost before it became too light.

West Beach was about a twenty-minute drive from Sarah's house. By the time Lawrence parked the car, the sun was already rising behind them. If it weren't so misty Tabi's Fish Bar would have cast a long shadow over the car park.

'Should we change into our wetsuits?' Lawrence asked.

'Later,' John said. 'I want to get up close and have a look at what we can see on the beach, first. I want to get a good look at the thing's face.'

They left their SCUBA gear in the car and headed towards the beach. John had his knife and his camera and a few other bits in a rucksack that he thought would be useful. He held onto the handrail as they walked down the stairs as the steps were slippery from the early morning fog. As they descended onto the beach the foul smell of the fish rose to meet them. John and Lawrence exchanged grimaces and carried on.

The monster was where they had left it. It was a pale shape in front of them, shrouded in a fine mist. John lifted his camera and took a photo. They were the only people on the beach. John and Lawrence walked towards it. The creature's head towered over them as they sidestepped the dead fish on the firm, wet sand.

John didn't think they would have too much time to properly examine the creature before it started to decay. If only he could bring a team over with him. His colleagues would jump at the chance to help with something like this. If he had Daphne Friedman and Bob Pohl working alongside him they would be able to examine the whole thing in a matter of days. However, Mitchell Miller had prohibited outsiders from getting involved and had left John with Lawrence, who was not just too young, but also under-experienced.

At least I have someone, John thought. *It would be a lot worse without any help at all.*

The sky darkened as heavy clouds drifted in to haunt the sky from the west. John was hoping that they'd have a clear sky and a nice day to look at the creature, but it was misty at the moment and now the dark clouds threatened rain. He hadn't bothered to bring a hat or a raincoat with him.

I'll deal with that if it happens, John thought. *And if worse comes to worst, I'll just put on my wetsuit.*

A swarm of seagulls were walking over the beach, looking at the dead fish in hungry disappointment. They had tried to peck at them but somehow knew that these fish weren't ripe for eating. The fish had washed ashore three mornings ago, and the birds were already starting to look thin.

'The gulls aren't even touching the creature,' Lawrence said.

'Would you want to eat it?' John asked.

'Maybe with some chips and curry sauce. We could take a slice over to Tabi's and see if she'd batter it for lunch.'

John laughed. 'I bet that would taste good,' he said but the combination of last night's whisky and the foul stench of the fish on the beach were starting to swirl in John's stomach and he began to feel a sour taste creep up the back of his throat. He swallowed, pushing the taste away. All he had that morning was a cup of tea and a biscuit and he suddenly felt like he could absolutely devour a hot, greasy bacon butty. His stomach started to rumble.

John looked up at the creature's eyes on the left side of its head, which were a few feet above him. It had one large eye and four smaller ones in a line behind it. Its smallest eye was the size of a human eyeball. The largest was four times larger than a football. It was perfectly round and domed. Despite the haziness that was beginning to form over its eyes, John could see that the iris of its largest eye was a dark silver colour, and it had specks in it that seemed to glint when they were looked at from the right angle, as though they really were made from silver. Its pupil, which had looked black and glossy yesterday, was clouding over with the signs of death.

What have you seen? John thought. *A creature of your size... swimming at the depths that you've reached... What have you seen?*

John took a photo. 'The eyes are more fish-like than serpentine,' John said. 'So, it's unlikely to be a type of water-serpent.'

'That's not normal, is it?' Lawrence asked. 'All those eyes.' He was standing as close as he could to the smaller eyes that trailed behind the main eye, looking up at them.

'Nothing about this is normal,' John said.

'Do other fish have multiple eyes?' Lawrence asked, not taking his own eyes off the creature's eyes.

'There's a deep-sea species that was recently discovered off the coast of New Zealand with four eyes,' John said. 'Two primary eyes on the top and two smaller ones on the sides.' He pointed to where the eyes would be on his own head. 'It has an almost three-sixty-degree view. Perfect for spotting predators. But it's hard to imagine that this thing has any predators.' *At least I hope it doesn't...* 'But these eyes could be something else. The smaller ones are different to its primary eyes.'

'How so?' Lawrence asked as he glanced from eye to eye.

'They don't have an iris. They might be for sensing something else, like the third parietal eye some sharks have.'

'You've lost me,' Lawrence said. 'What's a parietal eye?'

'It normally sits on top of their head,' John said, tapping the top of his own head, 'but it doesn't pick up images, just light. Kind of like a spider's eyes, they can pick up changes in light levels but not much else.'

'Do you think these eyes detected light, then?' Lawrence asked.

'Maybe a couple of them did,' John said. 'But the others could have been used to detect something completely different.' *Something otherworldly...* 'Have you ever heard of a mantis shrimp?' John asked.

'I may know how to dive but I don't know a thing about fish,' Lawrence said. 'So, you're going to have to explain a few things to me.'

'Well, mantis shrimp are these colourful shrimp, and their eyes are something special. Humans have three cones in their eyes, each one absorbs a different colour: red, green, and blue. So, our eyes can only pick up colours on the visible light spectrum because they're the colours that can be made by combining red, green and blue.'

'Oh,' Lawrence said. 'Like a TV.'

'Exactly like a TV,' John said. 'But some types of mantis shrimp have up to sixteen photoreceptors in their eyes. They are able to see colours that we don't even know *exist*.' He pointed to the creature's second smallest eye, which was the size of an apple, and said, 'They look a lot like this eye here, only much lighter in colour. I'd have to dissect it to know for certain, but I have a sneaking suspicion that this thing could see well-beyond our own spectrum of light. I'd bet good money that it could see properties that we don't even know exist.'

John took a photo of the eye and then jotted down a note so that he could follow up on it later. He then walked around to the front of the creature. Its teeth protruded neatly outside of its mouth. The two largest of which were nearly six-feet long and had serrated edges, like giant steak knives. The teeth were a yellowed ivory in colour, slightly aged from being exposed in the open water for its whole life.

'Look at these teeth,' John said in awe. He snapped a photo of them. 'Why would they need to be so big? And why the hell would they need to be serrated?'

'Maybe it eats sharks or whales?' Lawrence asked. 'Something big.'

'Could be,' John said. 'They don't look particularly well used though. They might just be for show... A deterrent or a defence.'

'What would it need to deter?' Lawrence asked.

'I have no idea,' John said as he lifted the creature's lip. It was heavy and smooth, like picking up a salmon fresh out of the water. It was too heavy to open it all the way, but he managed to open it far enough to catch a glimpse of the teeth inside.

'Get the torch out of my bag and shine it in here,' John said.

Lawrence grabbed the torch - a long Maglite - and shone it through the gap that John had opened. It had several rows of teeth inside, like a shark, each one cast sharp shadows in the part of the mouth that they could see. John lowered the lip and walked nearer to the end of the mouth. He cracked open the lip there. Lawrence shone the torch through the gap.

'Look at these ones,' John said, signalling to the smaller teeth at the back of the mouth. 'They have more signs of use. Look at this chip.' He pointed to a chunk missing from one of the teeth. The lip slipped in his hand, and John quickly put both hands back underneath it to stop it from dropping shut. 'These are the teeth it uses. But its mouth is so large I can't imagine it actually needs to chew anything. It could just swallow its prey whole.'

'Unless it needs to make sure it's dead,' Lawrence said. 'I wouldn't want to swallow a giant squid alive.'

'I'd like to see you try,' John said and laughed.

'Should you be touching it?' Lawrence asked.

'I don't know,' John said. 'Someone has to.'

John's biceps started to ache. He lowered the lip and placed his hand on the creature's skin. He walked around the head, sliding his hand over it as he went. Its large scales were smooth, like china plates, and there was a slight iridescence to them.

John imagined how it might shine, glow, or sparkle under an ultraviolet light.

Lawrence looked up at the sky. The sun had risen but it was getting darker. Most of the mist along the beach had dissipated but the clouds to the West were drawing in over them.

John felt small little bumps beneath the creature's skin as he walked around it. Then he stopped. He felt something large under his hand, something tough. He pressed down on it, and then around the lump. The lump was much firmer and offered more resistance than the skin around it. There was something lodged underneath its skin. Something hard. *Maybe the tooth of another creature?* John thought. *If it had gotten into a fight...*

'Come have a look at this,' he called to Lawrence, who was still marvelling at the creature's teeth. He had been sliding his hand up and down the part of a fang he could reach.

Lawrence went over to join him. 'What is it?' he asked.

'Feel this,' John said. He ran his hand over the lump on the side of the creature then gestured to Lawrence to do the same.

Lawrence frowned as he felt the lump. 'What is it?'

John took his knife out of his bag. It was a tactical knife with a dark green rubber handle. As he unsheathed it, he revealed the two sides of its blade. One side was sharp, like a sword, and the other side was serrated, like the creature's fangs.

'Let's find out,' John said.

He dug the knife deep into the skin and sawed around the lump, carving out a large chunk of flesh. The flesh was dark in colour and reeked of death.

'Not exactly roses, is it?' John said, grimacing. He crouched down on the sand and placed the chuck of flesh onto the beach. He carved away the excess flesh until he found the hard lump. He paused, looking at it in bemusement.

'What is it?' Lawrence asked again.

'It's metal,' John said. He continued carving bits of flesh away from the metal as though he were carving a statue from stone. He revealed the metal that had lodged into the flesh and continued to cut around it until he could remove it completely. He peeled away the last piece of flesh and dropped it to the ground. He walked over to where the water was lapping the shore and rinsed the piece of metal in water.

In his hand he held a spearhead. The metal was dark. Along the flat sides of the spearhead were intricate patterns that had been carved into the metal. They mirrored each other on either side of the central ridge, like butterfly wings.

'Is that a spearhead?' Lawrence asked.

John nodded. 'I believe so.'

So, humans have met you before? John thought. *Met you and tried to kill you.*

'Do you recognise these patterns?' John asked, showing them to Lawrence. They were intricately carved into the length of the metal.

Lawrence looked closer, not wanting to touch it. 'No, I don't,' he said. 'I've never seen anything like it before.'

'I think I have.' John lowered his voice as he pondered the frightening truth that the spearhead revealed. 'They're Viking... which means this thing must be...' John trailed off and looked up at the creature, trying to wrap his mind around this new discovery. From this angle the creature looked a lot taller. He felt a mix of awe and terror as he looked at its monstrous eyes. He turned the spearhead over in his hand again. The sides were as blunt as a spoon now, dulled by time. Any sign of the wooden part of the spear had long gone. Not even a splinter remained.

John turned back to Lawrence. He didn't know where to look. He felt like his eyes couldn't focus as his mind was trying to process the unfathomable. 'If these patterns really are Viking,' John said, 'then this spearhead has been stuck in that creature for over a thousand years…'

NINE

Flight will be blessed to the flightless.
From an ancient Hebridean prophecy.

Sarah Calvary sat at her kitchen table with the telephone to her ear. Its spiral cord stretched from her ear to the wall beside the fridge, where she kept the phone. The fridge had a few photos stuck to it, the most recent one of which was from Claire and Wallace's wedding from fifteen years ago. The rain was gently pattering against the window and the sky was a dark grey. Sarah had come home for lunch and to call a garage to see if they could replace her car's windscreen.

She was used to companies taking forever to answer her calls, but this time no sooner had she taken a sip of her tea, someone had answered the phone.

'Hello?' a man said.

Sarah quickly swallowed her mouthful of tea and put her mug down, causing a little bit of tea to spill over the lip of the mug and splatter onto the table.

'Hello,' Sarah said, then coughed as she tried to compose herself. 'I need someone to fix my windscreen. It's been—'

'Let me stop you there,' the man said. 'I need to transfer you to another department. Do you mind holding?'

'No, that's fine,' Sarah said, and risked another sip of tea. She sat upright and waited for them to speak again. Maybe it would take a while for someone to answer this time. She wiped away the spilled tea with a tissue.

Less than a minute later a man answered. 'Hello?'

'Yes, I was just saying to your colleague that I need someone to fix my windscreen and—'

'Your windscreen?' the man asked.

'Yes, it was broken.'

'Let me transfer you to the right department.'

'I thought someone had transferred me to the right department,' Sarah said.

'Can I put you on hold?'

Sarah let out a small sigh. 'Sure.'

Sarah looked outside and saw the rain now pouring down. Beads of water trickled down her windowpanes. She hoped that her windscreen wasn't leaking. She'd hate for her car to have water damage on top of everything else.

'Hello?' Yet another man answered the phone.

'Can you help me?' Sarah asked. 'My windscreen has been smashed.'

'What make is your car?' the man asked.

'A Ford. Is there any chance you can send someone to St. Budoc's Island to repair it this week?'

Sarah heard him type onto a keyboard. 'Hmm, we can't do it this week. We'll have to order it in especially.' He sounded uninterested.

'Do you know how long that will take?' Sarah asked.

She heard him typing again. *Tap tap tap.* 'It'll be here by next month.'

'Next month? But it's broken today. Next month isn't good enough,' Sarah said. She clenched her fist. 'Can you not just—'

'Sorry, can I put you on hold for a second?' he asked.

'No, I won't hold!' Sarah snapped. 'I've been put on hold twice already and... Hello? Hello?'

They had put her on hold. She threw the phone at the handset on the wall. The plastic on the phone cracked. As it swung, dangling from the cord, a small triangle of plastic fell from it.

'Ugh!' Sarah grunted. She'd have to get that replaced now too. She loved living on St. Budoc's Island, but she wished she could get replacements more easily. She had bought a Ford because she thought it was a common car, with easy-to-replace parts should it need to be repaired. Apparently, she was wrong. There was no such thing as 'easy-to-replace parts' on the island, not when everything had to be shipped in.

She dropped her head into her hands.

Ding-dong. The doorbell rang.

Sarah took a deep breath to try and calm herself down. She counted to three as she inhaled and counted to five as she exhaled. She didn't want whoever was at the door to see that she was mad. It was embarrassing.

Ding-dong.

'I'm coming,' she muttered. She stood up, hung the broken phone back on its mount, and went to open the front door. Standing outside, sopping wet and looking shaken, was Claire Burns. She had driven to Sarah's but in the time it had taken Sarah to answer the door, Claire had been soaked to the bone by the rain. She pushed past Sarah and walked into the house, dripping water across the floor.

'Is everything alright?' Sarah asked, closing the door behind her. She looked at Claire. She was a mess. Sarah could tell she'd been crying, even though the rain had mixed with her tears. Mascara was halfway down her face and her eyes were red.

'We have to go,' Claire said, matter-of-factly. She was trying to hold herself together but not succeeding.

'Hey, hey, it's alright,' Sarah said. 'Let me get you a towel so we can sit down.'

'There's no time,' Claire said. 'Just grab your things and let's go.'

'Go where?' Sarah asked.

'Anywhere,' Claire said. 'Away. Off this island.' Her desperation bled through her words. 'We can go to Glasgow, or Liverpool, or even London for all I care. We just need to go.'

'Let's just sit down and talk,' Sarah said. 'Would you like a cup of tea?' She led her into the kitchen, pulled a few tea towels out of a drawer, and handed them to Claire so she could dry herself.

Claire took them and wiped her face with one. Her mascara smeared across her cheeks towards her ears and stained the towel.

'Ever since that thing washed up on the beach something's been off,' Claire said. 'I can't put my finger on it, but something is wrong. It's not right.' She paced around the kitchen.

'What do you mean?' Sarah asked. She stood with her arms crossed, wrapping around herself like a comfort blanket.

'I want to leave,' Claire said. She stopped and stared at Sarah. 'I want *us* to leave. Wallace is working at the distillery. He doesn't have to know.'

'You want to leave Wallace?' Sarah asked and took a step towards her.

Claire shook her head. Her eyes welled up with tears. She dabbed at them with the stained towel. 'No,' she said. 'I don't. I begged him to come with me, but he won't listen to me. *"What about the distillery?"* he said. That's all he cares about. He wants to stay for his *precious* whisky.' There was so much spite in the way she said, *'precious'*. It made Sarah uncomfortable. Claire looked up at her with a pleading desperation in her eyes.

'I'm sorry, Claire,' Sarah said in a small voice. 'I can't leave.'

'Why?' Claire asked. 'This place has changed. That *thing* is seeing to it. It's changing people. No one's been the same since it washed up.'

'I know it's been hard. But things will get better.' Sarah took Claire's hand in her own and squeezed it. Claire looked down at their hands and then looked back up to Sarah's eyes.

'They won't,' Claire said.

'I promise you they will,' Sarah said, squeezing her hand again.

An almighty crack of thunder shook the house, causing Sarah to jump, and the windows rattled so hard that she thought they would shatter. With the thunder came an unholy downpour. The rain reached such an insane intensity that it sounded like gravel was being emptied onto the roof and thrown at the windows.

'Sarah!' Claire shouted. She let go of Sarah's hand, leapt out of her seat, and rushed to the window.

Sarah followed her. They both stood in utter shock as they looked at the downpour outside. At first, the rain looked like huge grey-green blurs falling past the window. Then Sarah realised that it wasn't rain that was falling from the sky.

It was fish.

TEN

The honey of the gods shall sour.
From an ancient Hebridean prophecy.

Fish rained down from the sky. The first fish smashed down into the sand next to John. The second one hit him on the head. That's when the thunder cracked and the dark sky unburdened its unholy load upon St. Budoc's Island. Fish after fish struck the beach around John and Lawrence, hitting the wet sand with intense slaps. Some exploded on impact, their guts bursting from their insides. Others hit the beach and slid along the slick, wet sand. Another fish hit John on the head. Its face struck John on the mouth as it spun from the impact and landed at his feet.

'Run!' John shouted. Both he and Lawrence ran across the beach, holding their arms above their heads for protection as they were pummelled with fish. The sand was hardening underfoot, making it increasingly difficult to run.

The noise was tremendous. The water was bombarded with fish as they splashed back into the sea. The assault of fish upon the beach sounded like a never-ending car crash. It was loud, raucous, and frightening.

'What's happening?' Lawrence yelled, but John couldn't hear him over the sound of the fish. The sky rumbled like a train as falling fish collided with each other mid-air, causing them to spiral as they hurtled towards the ground.

They made it to the car as Lawrence fumbled with his keys and unlocked it. They jumped in and John shut his door as quickly as possible, but Lawrence caught a fish in his door and had to reopen it to let the fish fall to the floor. They took a second to catch their breath and focus before they looked at each other in total confusion. They were both soaked. Fish bounced off the roof and the windscreen. To John, it sounded like being in a cheap car wash at a rundown petrol station, as the giant blue brushes beat against the car. A fish the size of a salmon struck the car roof and left a dent.

'Oh crap,' Lawrence said. He pushed the dent as hard as he could but couldn't pop it back out. Another fish struck the windscreen and cracked it. They were falling hard and fast.

'Damn it!' Lawrence shouted.

'Drive!' John yelled.

Lawrence started the engine and raced away from the beach. His window wipers could barely keep up against the rain and were almost useless against the fish. A few small fish got caught at the bottom, where the windscreen met the bonnet. One fish hit the windscreen and exploded, spraying its guts over the glass. The window wipers smeared it, turning the windscreen opaque and for a second Lawrence couldn't see where he was going. As the rain quickly washed the innards away it revealed the onslaught of yet more fish falling in front of him.

Another fish struck the windscreen and left a larger crack on the passenger's side, which startled Lawrence and caused him to hit a large fish in the middle of the road, sending the car into a spin. Lawrence lost control. As the car spun, John was pushed into the door by the force. A second later Lawrence managed to regain control and kept the car going straight, narrowly avoiding a collision with a stone wall.

Well saved, John thought, too stunned to speak.

They stopped when they got to the Mariner's Dog. There was a small tree outside which provided a laughable amount of shelter, but Lawrence parked beneath it anyway, as it was the closest shelter to the pub. The rest of the island must have had the same idea as John and Lawrence because when they ran into the pub, a crowd of people were crammed in the doorway, watching the fish fall from the sky. Many more were squeezed beside each other inside, looking out of the windows.

'Let us through!' John shouted and they pushed past the people blocking the doorway. John felt immediate relief when they were inside the pub, but the noise inside wasn't any better. The fish were hitting the roof, causing some of the tiles to slide off and smash onto the pavement.

'What's going on?' Angus shouted, straining his neck to look out the window from behind the bar.

Most of the fish falling past the window were dead. If they weren't dead when they fell, then they were when they struck the ground. The air was thick with their stench. A few of them managed to survive and thrashed violently in the puddles on the ground. *What a shock,* John thought. It was scary enough for him, he could only imagine how traumatised the fish were. One minute they were swimming in the sea, minding their own business, and the next they were hurtling through the sky and falling to the ground.

John and Lawrence were soaked through to the skin. Their clothes clung to them like papier-mâché as they stood there shivering, both wishing they had taken a coat with them when they left that morning. But a fish storm isn't the kind of thing they forecast on the morning news.

'What the hell was that?' Lawrence asked, forcing his way to a window to watch the rest of the fish fall from the sky.

Wallace Burns was working inside his distillery when the fish started to fall. Two large copper stills stood in the centre of the distillery. To Wallace, it just sounded like heavy rain hitting the roof, but when he opened the door to look outside, he was horrified to see the falling fish.

His distillery was mostly surrounded by grass, and the soft ground meant that more of the fish survived the fall. The grass became alive with the hopeless flailing of fish, gasping for a fresh breath of water. Their wild eyes and gaping mouths looked like they were drowning. And in a way, they were.

Wallace was petrified at the sight of the fish. He shook his head and stepped back, muttering to himself, 'It's happening... it's happening... it's happening...' over and over again.

He turned and ran to the far end of the distillery, opened the wooden door to the basement, and headed down the wooden stairs to where he was ageing his whisky. Rows and rows of barrels lined the basement. He had different types of barrels for the different batches of whisky that he was working on. Some were being aged in oak, some in American bourbon barrels, and he was even trying to age a couple in old sherry casks. Wallace had invested years of study and experimentation into his craft, and was known not just around the island, but around the country, for the quality of his whisky.

Wallace grabbed a small whisky glass from an antique cabinet and frantically turned the tap on one of the barrels. Whisky gushed out, filling the glass. He shut it off, took a sip of the whisky and instantly spat it out. It was disgusting.

'No!' Wallace shouted. Spit and whisky sprayed from his mouth.

The whisky had turned. The honey and heather notes had been replaced with an acrid, bitter taste that he couldn't quite place, and the beautiful amber colour was now cloudy and unpleasant. His whisky had become repulsive.

Wallace marched to the next barrel and filled the glass with whisky.

'Come on...' he begged. 'Come on...'

The whisky rushed out from the tap and poured all over his hand. He could smell the rancid liquid before he tasted it, but took a sip anyway, just to make sure. As soon as the whisky passed through his lips, he spat it straight out across the floor. He couldn't describe it. It wasn't just sour and bitter... it was fishy.

'No!' he yelled. His face became a dark red as blood rushed to his head. His temples throbbed in agony. 'No!!'

He grabbed another clean glass from the cabinet and rushed down to the end of the row of barrels, feet slapping against the concrete floor. Maybe the second barrel only tasted bad because he had used the same glass... maybe all he needed was a clean one. At the far end of the rows of barrels sat a very special whisky that he'd been ageing for almost a quarter of a century. He remembered barrelling it when he first started to work at the distillery. He had just turned twenty and his dad had suggested he reach out to old Michael Argyle to see if he would offer him an apprenticeship. Since then, he had bought the distillery from Michael Argyle after he had retired and had turned it into what it was today. On the barrel was a small sign that said, 'Twenty-Five Year,' with the date on which it would be bottled. It was due to be bottled the first week of July: less than two months away.

He took a deep, nervous breath to calm his nerves, and steadied himself with one hand on the barrel. The glass trembled in his other hand with fearful anticipation.

'Please, please, please...' he said, as if praying to the whisky itself.

He held the glass beneath the tap and opened it just enough to allow a few dark amber drops to fall into the glass. If, by the grace of God, it was still good he couldn't afford to waste any of it. He swirled the whisky in the glass and then lifted it to his nose to smell. He gently shook his head as the fishy aroma filled his nose, and his eyes began to fill with tears.

'Please...' he whispered, as though begging would change anything.

He took a sip of the whisky and spat it out with a scream. His face turned a darker shade of beetroot. Twenty-five years of whisky was wasted. Wallace's life's work was in these barrels and it now reeked of rotten fish. He threw the glass to the ground. It shattered, shooting tiny shards of glass over the floor. He looked across the row of barrels, as he burned with desperate rage. He knew what was happening. He knew the implications. He had read about it himself.

'It's really happening,' he said.

'I'm going home to pack my bags,' Claire Burns said to Sarah Calvary. They were still in Sarah's kitchen, looking at the dead fish on the ground outside. The rain had died down now to just a drizzle and the fish had stopped falling. 'Wallace is still at work. I can take the keys to his boat without him knowing. Then I'll come back for you to see if you've changed your mind. I hope you will, Sarah. For your sake as much as mine.'

'I'll think about it,' Sarah said, but she had already made up her mind. She wasn't going anywhere. She was born on this island and she was planning to die on this island.

'Don't think for too long,' Claire said. 'I'll be back in an hour.' She gave Sarah a hug and kissed her on both cheeks. 'Pack your bags.'

Claire got into her car and drove through the rain, with both hands on the steering wheel, carefully trying to avoid the fish. Occasionally one would flop in the road and startle her. She drove slowly around them, not wanting to squish them. There weren't any other cars on the road.

It took her fifteen minutes longer to get home than usual. She parked in her driveway and went inside, noticing that Wallace's car was still gone and thought that he must still be at work.

Wallace kept the keys to his boat on the top shelf of their liquor cabinet. The cabinet was full of whisky, mainly various batches of St. Budoc's whisky that they had produced over the years, but there were a few other special bottles that had been gifts for various birthdays and anniversaries too.

Claire grabbed the keys and went upstairs to pack her bag. She only needed to take a few things with her: enough clothes and money to get her by until she could figure out what she should do, and a few sentimental essentials, like her mother's photo album, because she decided there and then that when she left, she was never, ever going to return to St. Budoc's.

John and Lawrence were sat at a table in the Mariner's Dog. Ben Walters came and joined them. He was in a slight daze, as were most people inside the pub.

'It's crazy, isn't it?' Ben said as he sat down with them, holding a glass of whisky.

'I've never seen it in person,' John said. 'I've heard about it before though. I just never thought I'd see it with my own eyes.'

'This has happened before?' Lawrence asked.

'It happens more often than you'd expect, maybe once every few years, but I've never heard of it happening in Scotland before. Heavy winds pick up a load of fish, they get sucked up into the clouds and can be transported for miles,' John told them. 'Ancient civilisations thought it was a sign of the end times.'

'Should we be worried?' Ben asked.

John laughed. 'We should just be glad it wasn't raining snakes.'

'*That* happens?' Lawrence asked and grimaced. 'God, maybe it is the end times.'

John chuckled, but Ben kept his head down, looking into his whisky with a solemn expression.

'Hey Lawrence, do you mind giving Ben and me a minute to talk?'

'Sure,' he said, standing up. 'Would you like a drink?'

'No thanks,' John said.

'I've got one,' Ben said, lifting his head and gesturing to the whisky in his hands.

Lawrence headed over to the bar and ordered a drink from Angus. Angus was more interested in what was happening outside but poured him a glass of Coke.

Ben took a sip of his whisky and immediately spat it back into the glass.

'No good?' John asked.

Ben wiped his tongue with his sleeve and grimaced. He called over to Angus, 'What's this piss you're serving?' Angus didn't hear him. He was preoccupied with another patron, who was also complaining about their whisky.

'Ben,' John said. 'I saw your father last night.'

'You did?' Ben asked as he swirled the whisky inside his glass and inspected it.

'He was waiting outside Sarah's house when we got home,' John said. 'He had smashed Sarah's car windscreen and then threatened me.'

Ben lowered his head. 'I'm so sorry, John. He hasn't been the same since Patrick died.'

'None of us have,' John said.

'He took to the bottle shortly after,' Ben said. 'But with everything that's going on here, I don't think he's the only one who'll be turning to drink.' He looked at his glass; he was about to take another sip and then quickly remembered that he'd just spat the whisky back into the glass. He pushed it away from himself.

An open suitcase sat on the bed Claire Burns shared with her husband. She opened her wardrobe and grabbed a few essential items of clothing - summer and winter tops, trousers, a dress – and threw them into the case. She grabbed a pair of running shoes from the bottom of the wardrobe and stuffed them in there too.

She opened the bottom drawer of her chest of drawers. There was a thick envelope. She opened it to peer inside. It contained over a thousand pounds in notes. Wallace always kept a large amount of cash that he refused to put in the bank, so he didn't have to declare it with the rest of his earnings. It wasn't the only envelope of cash stashed away in the house and Claire suspected that he had even more cash hidden at the distillery that he didn't want her to know about.

She took out the cash, stuffed it into the suitcase, and then padded the envelope out with a pair of socks. It wouldn't take Wallace long to discover that the cash was missing, but she hoped it would at least buy her some time.

She grabbed her jewellery box from the top of the dresser and took out the necklace her mother had given to her to wear for her wedding, which her mother had also worn for hers, and her grandmother's wedding ring, which she slipped onto the ring finger of her right hand.

The front door clicked open downstairs. She froze, listening. Wallace had come home.

She flipped the lid of the suitcase shut and locked it, then she stuffed it into the wardrobe and prayed that Wallace wouldn't look inside. She rearranged a few dresses that were hanging up in the wardrobe so they'd hide it.

'Hello?' she called downstairs. A slight tremor cracked her voice. Maybe he didn't know that she was home… Or maybe he expected her to be home and came to check up on her after he saw the raining fish.

She heard him walk up the stairs. They creaked beneath his feet as he climbed. Claire saw that she had left the bottom drawer open so she quietly shut it with her foot, hiding the sock-padded envelope inside.

'Wallace?' she called again.

He swung open the door to the bedroom, and she stared at him in shock. All the life had drained from his pale face. His eyes looked glossy and unfocused, as though he was constantly looking into the distance. Something was terribly wrong.

Did he know that she was planning to leave? No… He couldn't have. Claire had only decided to leave that day. There was no way he would have known. Unless Sarah had spoken to him...

'Wallace, I was just—'

BANG.

Wallace cut her off with a shotgun. She had been so preoccupied with her own secrets that she hadn't even noticed him carrying the gun in his arms. The pellets tore through her chest and abdomen, spraying blood across the wall behind her. She stumbled backwards and hit the floor. The sound of the gun echoed throughout the house. Outside the window, a flock of birds suddenly took to the sky.

Claire looked up at Wallace. He was a blur to her. Blood trickled out of her mouth. Her vision reddened. Had blood covered her eyes? The thought was cut short as her body lurched in agonising pain.

'I'm sorry, Claire,' Wallace said. 'Have you seen what's happening to this place?' He crouched down in front of her and grabbed her chin in his rough hands. He turned her face so he could look at her. 'There's no hope for any of us.'

Claire looked past her husband to a twenty pound note that had fallen out of her suitcase onto the floor. Out of the window she saw the birds flying away in the distance. Rather than flying, though, they seemed to be swimming. Claire's body was on fire, yet she felt as if she were slipping into dark water. She wondered if she was swimming too.

ELEVEN

As the master sleeps, the servant prepares.
An old Hebridean proverb.

The doors to the Mariner's Dog slammed open, hitting a man on the other side.

'Argh!' he shouted as he clutched his shoulder.

A distraught woman ran in, screaming. John and Lawrence turned to look, along with everyone else. She was wearing a coat and a long corduroy skirt. Her hair looked like snakes, winding out from all angles.

'Mitchell Miller! Is he here?' she shouted.

Lawrence stood up. 'What's wrong?' he asked.

'Wallace has gone insane,' she said, struggling to catch her breath. 'He's walking through town with a shotgun. I just saw him shoot at a car.'

'Angus!' Lawrence yelled. 'The phone!' He ran over to the bar. Angus passed him the landline and dropped it on the bar in front of him. Lawrence pounded in his uncle's phone number. The phone rang.

'Is anyone hurt?' Angus asked the woman from behind the bar.

'I don't know,' she told him. 'But he's covered in blood.'

'Mitchell?' Lawrence said as Mitchell answered his phone. 'Get down to the Mariner's Dog. Bring your gun.'

Wallace Burns meandered through the town, slowly walking down the high street, unsure as to where he should go. He turned one direction and took a few steps before changing his mind and walked in another direction. He kicked away a dying fish that was twitching in front of him. It hit the side of a car that was parked on the side of the road– several fish lay dead or dying on the car's roof.

Wallace kept his shotgun held out in front of him at all times. He was on high alert.

A butcher peered out of his shop window and saw Wallace waving the gun around. Wallace caught sight of him and turned his gun to face the shop. The butcher's eyes widened like a deer in headlights when he saw the blood on Wallace's shirt and the mania in his eyes. He dropped down behind the counter.

Wallace pulled the trigger and the window exploded. Glass rained down over the butcher, tinkling as it hit the ground.

'Don't shoot!' the butcher yelled from inside, pulling himself into a ball. He brought his legs up closer to his body and lowered his head. 'Please, don't shoot!'

Wallace pumped the shotgun and fired again. This time the pellets shattered the glass display cabinet and tore through the meat inside, spraying raw meat all over the shop. The butcher jolted as the second shot fired. He wasn't sure if he should try to crawl away before Wallace found him or if he should stay hidden behind the counter, but before he could decide he heard Wallace pull two more shells out of his pockets and begin to reload the shotgun.

Wallace slotted the shells into place, clicked the gun shut, and pumped it one more time, but instead of turning the gun on the butcher, he turned around and continued on his journey, leaving the butcher cowering behind the counter.

As he walked away from the butcher's, Wallace spotted The Mariner's Dog. Suddenly he felt a sense of clarity, and no longer meandered through the town, but made a beeline straight for the pub. He now had a destination.

Ben saw Wallace heading towards them. 'Everyone, out back!' he called, stepping away from the window and shaking his hand in the direction of the back door. Angus opened it to let everyone out into the beer garden at the back of the pub. Everyone rushed together, pushing their way through. It was pandemonium. Someone yelled as they were squashed against the bar. A woman tripped and would have fallen to the floor if it weren't for Angus who had managed to grab hold of her before she fell.

John stood next to Ben, watching as Wallace picked up speed.

'What are you doing?' Ben muttered, wondering out loud.

John suddenly saw the giant sea creature in his mind. It was lying dead on the beach, surrounded by thousands of dead fish. It may be dead, but its eyes glistened as though it could see John… as though it could see Wallace with his gun… as though it could see everything. John felt as if he was being watched. He might not know what was happening but someone knew… some*thing* knew.

John's thoughts had distracted him for the few moments it took Wallace to approach the pub, and he was now standing outside the window. Ben grabbed hold of John's arm and yanked him to the ground just as Wallace fired into the pub. The windows shattered and everyone left inside the pub screamed. John covered his head as the glass fell over him. His knees suddenly surged with pain as he realised that he had landed on them when Ben pulled him to the ground.

'Quickly!' Angus yelled to the people trying to rush out. He used his hand to push them out even faster. 'As quick as you can!'

The pub door burst open yet again. Wallace marched inside and glanced over the pub and at the people rushing out the back door, with his gun in hand.

Ben jerked around to look at Wallace, standing between him and the last few patrons scrambling to get out the back door.

John was still crouching by the window, frozen to the spot. Lawrence, Angus, and a few others stayed behind to watch from various places they thought were safe. Curiosity and a sense of obligation had gotten the better of their immediate need for safety.

'It's awake,' Wallace said, staring into Ben's eyes. He was sweating and shaking. 'It's coming for us. All the signs are there. It's awake.'

'Wallace,' Ben said calmly, holding out his hands in front of him as though he were warding off a rabid dog. 'I'm going to need you to put the gun down.'

'It's over,' Wallace said. He was crying now. 'Everything's over. It's all over.'

'What's over?' Ben asked. 'Nothing's over. Everything is fine, Wallace.' He kept his voice soft and moved as little as possible. He was trying not to startle Wallace. As long as he had the gun in his hands, Wallace couldn't be trusted.

'The whisky!' Wallace yelled, looking more like a mad dog than ever. 'The whisky's turned! Dying like this is better than the pain to come. You know this, Ben. You *know* this!'

'What pain, Wallace? What's to come?' Ben asked. 'You're just spooked. We all are. The creature on the beach, the fish... we're all spooked. That's it.'

'Don't pretend,' Wallace spat. His face was surging with hatred. 'You *know*.'

Angus slowly rose from his safe place behind the bar with his hands in the air. 'Ben's right, Wallace,' Angus said as calmly as he could. 'There's nothing to be afraid of.' He nodded along with Ben. 'It was just a wee bit of rain. Everything is going to be—'

BANG.

Wallace shot him in the head. Skin ripped from Angus' face and several pellets exploded bottles sitting on the shelves. A split-second later, Angus crashed into the shelves behind him, causing even more bottles of whisky to shatter as they hit the floor. Their sour stench erupted into the pub and became tangled with the smell of gunpowder.

'No!' Ben yelled.

John reflexively reached toward Angus as he fell, but the movement caught Wallace's eye, and he spun around and pointed his gun at him. John's breath caught in his throat. The ends of the two barrels were perfect circles and he was staring right into them. If dying meant seeing a light at the end of the tunnel, then these tunnels only showed darkness. John started to raise his own hands in the air. Fear surged through his body and his heart was pounding so hard that his heartbeat distorted his vision.

'You never should have come back here,' Wallace said, shaking his head. He cocked his gun, steadied it, and fired.

Click.

Nothing.

The gun was empty.

Wallace cracked the barrel and pulled a handful of shells from his pocket, dropping some on the floor as he tried to reload with shaking hands. They rolled and rattled across the pub floor until they hit chair and table legs. John's heart skipped a beat and for a moment he thought he was about to pass out but a shot of adrenaline ripped through his body instead.

Before Wallace could finish reloading, John leapt from behind the table and charged at him. His shoulder crashed into Wallace's windpipe and knocked him to the ground. They landed with a thud and John felt his skeleton rattle and his heart leap out of his chest. There was a sound like a hammer hitting a coconut as Wallace's head hit the floor. Blood pooled around the back of his head like a dark halo and his eyes floated around their sockets in a daze. John quickly spun him around, pushed the gun away from him, and pressed his face into the pub's wooden floor. He sat on his back, grabbed hold of Wallace's hands, and held them behind him to ensure that he couldn't make any sudden movements. With a head injury like that, he wasn't sure that he'd be able to move at all, but there was no way that John was going to risk it.

Mitchell stormed into the pub, sweating and out of breath. He pointed his gun into the pub and at John and then down at Wallace.

'It's awake, Ben,' Wallace said in a dazed slur with half of his mouth sputtering against the blood-soaked floor. 'It's awake…'

John replayed the events over and over in his mind as Lawrence drove him home. First, he thought of the Viking spearhead, that hand-sized piece of metal that had been stuck in the creature with the intricate pattern carved into it. He remembered from school that the Vikings existed between the ninth and eleventh century and had occupied the Hebrides from about 1079. That meant the spearhead could have been lodged in the creature for over a thousand years, unless someone more recently was hunting with antique weapons. But judging by how well the creature's skin had healed and built up around the spearhead, it seemed unlikely that it had been attacked recently. At least not by the Vikings.

Lawrence was driving much slower now. He carefully manoeuvred around the fish carcasses that littered the road. Any of them that were alive when they fell were now dead. A rancid smell floated across the island. It was putrid enough to cling to the inside of John's nostrils. There was no escaping it.

Next, John's mind turned to the fish. He'd heard of fish raining from the sky. He'd read about it happening in Sri Lanka and in India, but not in Scotland. It normally occurred when whirlwinds formed over shallow water and created a waterspout that sucked the fish, and whatever other creatures were unlucky enough to be there, up into the swarming clouds.

The water around us is too deep, John thought. *If it's deep enough to keep a giant sea monster hidden for however many centuries it had been alive, then it would certainly be too deep for fish to be sucked up by a waterspout...*

John remembered seeing old sailing maps with illustrations of giant lobsters, or dragons attacking ships. *Here be monsters...* He had put it down to drunk sailors misunderstanding giant squids or other creatures, like how sailors mistook manatees for mermaids. But now John started to wonder if there was more truth to those stories than he had expected. Maybe sailors really had encountered these giant monsters and put them on their maps to warn other boats. Maybe their tales weren't so tall after all. The giant squid, or the kraken, had been nothing more than a mythological monster for hundreds of years, but in 1873 fishermen off the coast of Newfoundland cut off the tentacle of a creature as it was attacking their boat and brought it back to shore to be photographed. The giant squid stepped out of mythology and into the science books. Maybe the same was true for the other monsters and dragons that decorated those old maps.

John's mind then drifted to Wallace Burns. *What had he been saying? 'It's awake?' What's awake?* John thought. *The creature?*

When John saw it earlier it was dead, without a shadow of a doubt. He had smelled the flesh he had cut from its cheek and nothing alive smelled that awful.

Wallace had gone insane. That's the only logical explanation. Why would anyone else stalk a high street toting a shotgun?

It's awake.

It has to be connected, John thought. *It all has to be connected somehow.*

'What's connected?' Lawrence asked. He was tightly gripping the steering wheel of his Mini, making sure that he wouldn't drive faster than fifteen miles an hour.

'Huh?' John said, suddenly pulled out of his thoughts.

'You said, "It has to be connected..."' Lawrence repeated.

'Oh,' John said. 'I didn't realise I'd said that out loud.'

'Do you think the creature on the beach and the raining fish are connected somehow?' Lawrence asked.

'I think so,' John said. 'I just don't know how. My gut is telling me that they must be... but scientifically I'm not so sure.'

'And what about Wallace? Is he connected to it too?'

Lawrence pulled up outside Sarah's house. The sky was clear now, and a pale shade of blue. The dark clouds had blown away over the sea, maybe to drop the remaining fish elsewhere. John didn't answer.

'So... see you tomorrow, then?' Lawrence asked.

'I guess so,' John said. 'If you're not scared off?'

'I'd be lying if I said that I wasn't scared,' Lawrence said. 'But if you think we might be able to figure out what's going on, it's too important not to continue.'

John nodded and took his small bag inside with him but left his SCUBA gear in the car. Lawrence told him to leave it, since they'd be needing it in the morning anyway.

John unlocked the door to the house. Before anything else, he heard Sarah sobbing in the living room. He stepped inside and pressed his back against the wall in the entryway, closed his eyes and took a deep breath in. He slowly exhaled before peering into the living room. Sarah was on her side, lying down on the sofa. A blanket was pulled over her and a hundred used tissues were scrunched up and discarded on the floor beneath her head.

She looked up as she heard John. Snot covered her upper lip and her eyes were red.

John sat down beside her and she rearranged herself to sit up. He put his arm around her so she could nestle into him.

'I saw her,' Sarah said. 'Before she was killed, she was here…'

'Claire?' John asked. But he already knew. When Mitchell Miller had arrived at the pub, he had explained to them what had happened – or at least as much as he was willing to share. That's what took him so long to get there. He had been called to Claire and Wallace's house by a concerned neighbour who had heard the shot. The island only had a few police officers, and they were all locals. Hardly anything happened, and when something did happen, rarely would more than one thing happen in a day.

'She wanted me to leave with her,' Sarah continued.

'Leave the island?' John asked.

She nodded. 'If I said yes, she'd still be alive.' She started to cry again. John looked around and saw that the box of tissues was completely empty. He grabbed the cleanest tissue he could find in the pile and handed it to her. She took it, scrunched it up, and just held it to her face as she sobbed.

'Or you might both be dead. You can't blame yourself, Sarah,' John said. 'What happened was awful but it wasn't your fault.'

'I don't know how people do it,' Sarah said. She spoke softly with a slight soreness to her throat. 'I can't cope with loss. I wanted to die when Mum and Dad passed.' She looked up at him and said, 'It was even worse when you left.'

'I'm sorry,' John said. 'I didn't have a choice.'

'You didn't even say goodbye,' Sarah said. 'When Patrick died you just got up and left. I didn't know where you were. I didn't know where you were heading. For all I knew, they'd killed you too.'

John stiffened and took his arm off of her. 'And who are *"they"*?' he said, standing up. 'No one was ever arrested for his death. He was murdered on this godforsaken island, with only a handful of people, and no one was caught? No one was arrested? Someone knows who killed him.'

'Did you see who killed him?' Sarah asked.

John didn't want to talk about this. Since he had run away, he'd tried to keep that day blocked out of his mind, and out of his nightmares. He knew coming back to St. Budoc's would open up his most fragile wound.

No, he thought. *Not open, rip.* Open was too gentle of a word. He had managed to keep it closed for so long – it had taken him years to overcome that pain – but now it was all he could think of.

'It was thirty years ago,' John said. 'They drugged us. I've given myself migraines trying to remember what happened. If it weren't for me, he'd still be alive and we might still be…'

John trailed off. He was doing the exact thing he had told Sarah not to do. He was blaming himself for Patrick's death.

'You'd still be what?' Sarah asked. She looked into his eyes, urging him to open up to her. 'Together?'

TWELVE

The old shall replace the new.
From an ancient Hebridean prophecy.

'Do you still want to examine it today?' Lawrence asked as John buckled his seatbelt. It was still dark and, as always, a thin cloak of mist hovered over the island.

'I don't think we have a choice,' John said. After his argument with Sarah, he couldn't fall asleep. He kept thinking about everything that had happened that day. *It has to be connected,* he reminded himself. Maybe by studying the creature he could uncover answers. Or maybe there weren't any answers to be uncovered. Maybe the creature was just a new species, the rain of fish was just an isolated phenomenon, and Wallace had just lost his mind. Maybe they weren't connected at all... John urged himself to think rationally, but something was gnawing at the back of his mind and he didn't think it would go away until he found some answers.

Lawrence put the car into gear and drove to West Beach, crouching down to look through the parts of the windscreen that were still intact. As the sun rose, and the mist began to dissipate, John saw an old man, in his suit, out in his front garden picking up the fish that had fallen and throwing them into a bucket. *He's going to need a bigger bucket,* John thought.

Lawrence had turned the heater in the car on full blast. Hot air rattled out of the car's little fans. The warmth was nice but the air carried a faint smell of fish. John wondered if some of yesterday's fishy rainwater had somehow gotten inside the fans. He tilted the fan away from his face. It seemed like he'd smelt nothing but fish since being back on the island.

John and Lawrence unloaded their gear in the car park. Tabi's Fish Bar stood at the other end of the car park. Near the entrance he saw an unhealthily skinny seagull pluck rubbish out of the bin, looking for something to eat. Tabi's lights were off at the moment but come lunchtime there would be people queuing up to eat their fish and chips and pickled eggs. Right now, however, the car park was empty. It was just the two of them in the morning haze.

'Let's suit up,' John said and pulled his wetsuit out of his case. It hadn't been able to completely dry since he'd gone diving with his students. He should have hung it up to dry when he got to Sarah's, but the chaos of the last few days meant he'd forgotten. Now it was uncomfortably cold and smelled faintly of mildew.

'Here?' Lawrence asked.

'There's no one about,' John said as he glanced around the car park. 'Just turn around.' He would have preferred a changing room or a toilet or something to change in, but with none of them available, John just had to pretend that he was by himself. He still felt awkward about changing though and if Lawrence had a larger car John would have asked if he could change in there instead.

They each took a side of the car and undressed, facing away from each other. The cool air raised goosebumps on John's skin. He neatly folded his clothes as he removed them and placed them on the passenger seat of Lawrence's Mini. As he laid them down, he saw that Lawrence had already removed his shirt, through the open car door. Lawrence's back was pale and toned, speckled with several moles that formed a constellation on his back. He stepped out of his...

...trousers and laid them on the bench in front of him. Suddenly John was seventeen again, standing in the old changing room. It was full of boys getting ready for their PE lesson. John unbuttoned his white shirt and hung it on the hook behind him. He saw Patrick across the changing room. Patrick smiled at him. It stirred the butterflies inside of John's stomach. Patrick turned away as he took off his shirt and unzipped his grey school-trousers. They slid down his pale legs and he stepped out of them before hanging them next to his shirt.

'Oi, John,' a cocky boy John could barely remember said. He was nothing but a blur in this memory. The boy nudged his friend and nodded towards John.

John turned around and looked at him.

'It's rude to point,' the boy said.

John looked down at his underwear, which stretched out at the front. Embarrassment flooded through him. He grabbed his bag and held it in front of himself to hide his shame. The boy lunged toward him and yanked it away, throwing it across the changing room and almost hitting another boy in the face. John felt the pain...

...resurface inside of him. The pain of the past was strong. John was pulled back into the present and immediately jerked his eyes away from

Lawrence, who was now fully suited up in his wetsuit. He felt dizzy. He placed his hand on top of the car to steady himself.

'What's taking so long?' Lawrence asked, as he turned to look at John.

John finished putting on his wetsuit and took his SCUBA gear out of the case. The wetsuit was difficult to put on because it was damp. The cold caused John to erupt in goosebumps. He knew it'd be fine once he got into the water but at the moment, this early in the morning, it was unbearable. Once they were ready, the pair of them carried their gear down the stairs and onto the beach.

The creature lay behind them as John and Lawrence carried out their final checks, checking their Buoyancy Control Devices, weights, and air. When they were satisfied that everything was in order, they put on their flippers and awkwardly walked backwards into the water, taking long, difficult steps as they tried to avoid tripping over their flippers.

The chill of the water shocked John as it flooded his wetsuit. It shocked him more than he expected, seeing as he was already frozen to the bone. It was a shock that he had never gotten used to and wasn't convinced that anyone ever did. Before long, his body gradually brought the water in his suit up to temperature and he was finally comfortable and warm.

Dead fish floated on the surface of the water around them. A lot of fish had washed ashore, but the tide had taken some of them back out with it. As they backed into the sea, they gently pushed the fish away from them. Seagulls floated next to the fish, occasionally pecking at them but never eating them. There were fewer gulls today, and the gulls that remained looked worse-for-wear.

When the water was up to his waist, John pulled his goggles over his eyes. His waterproof camera hung from his wrist and his knife was in its sheath and secured to his belt. He never dived without it.

'Ready?' John asked.

'Ready,' Lawrence replied.

They inserted their mouthpieces. The tough rubber filled John's mouth. He checked his oxygen one last time, making sure it was still good, and breathed deeply before submerging himself completely.

The water had a deep, almost greenish hue to it. Sand, rocks, and seaweed were scattered along the seabed along with some of the fish that had sunk to the bottom. Other fish were falling from the surface. They almost looked like they were suspended in mid-air. John knocked one out of his way and it spun away in slow-motion. The visibility was better than John had expected. He could see about fifteen metres in front of himself before the water became too hazy.

John and Lawrence swam side-by-side. John pointed towards the submerged body of the creature and then swam towards it. They could just about make out the shape beyond the haze. Occasionally their flippers would hit a sinking fish and it would catch them off guard. It was another added difficulty that they really didn't need.

The body of the creature became clearer as they swam towards it. John lifted his camera and took a photo. The camera was in a watertight yellow case. The flash above the lens illuminated the creature, which rested on the seafloor. They couldn't see its tail. That was lost a long way away in the haze, further out – and probably deeper – than they were planning on diving to today. John wondered what type of tail it would have. Would it be vertical, like a fish, or horizontal, like a whale? Or maybe it would just taper to a point like that of a sea snake. He suspected that it would be more like that of a fish. He'd already ruled the creature out as being serpentine, and it definitely wasn't mammalian. Yet he couldn't see any gills on the creature, suggesting that it breathed air instead of water, or at least as well as water. Maybe it was a new class altogether.

John swam closer to the monster until he could touch it. He placed his hand on its side so that he could feel its skin. He couldn't feel much through his gloves, so he lifted the base of his glove to free his thumb. He stroked the monster's skin. It was slick and smooth and felt as though it was covered with a thin, mucousy membrane, like that of a hydrated chia seed. Its skin above water didn't feel like this, so maybe this was some kind of protective layer. Similar to how John's wetsuit was designed to keep him warm, maybe this was to protect the creature from the cold depths of the sea.

As John moved his hand over the creature's skin, he wondered if there were any other Viking weapons lodged into it, waiting to be discovered.

Viking, or older... he thought.

John pulled his thumb back into the glove and then turned to Lawrence. He signalled for Lawrence to follow him. They swam along the length of the creature's body as they went deeper into the sea.

It was bigger than John could have possibly imagined. It could have eclipsed a basking shark and made it look like a guppy.

It must have come from the deep, John thought. *Somewhere down in the depth of the ocean. A world where humans have barely begun to explore.*

After swimming for a couple of minutes, they lost sight of the creature's head. For about fifteen metres in either direction it was just a colossal body. No head, no tail. *Does this creature have an end?*

John noticed a strange mark on its side and gestured for Lawrence to come towards him. A circular wound, about a metre in diameter, looked as though it had been carved into the creature's skin with a sharp blade.

John snapped a photo of it. The flash illuminated the wound. It didn't look like it had time to heal before the creature died.

John placed his hand in the centre of the wound to take a photo but couldn't get the camera far enough back to capture the whole mark. He gestured for Lawrence to come over. John took Lawrence's hand and placed it in the centre of the mark, then swam back until he was far enough away to photograph the whole wound with Lawrence's hand for scale. John raised his camera and took a photo. When the flash went off John suddenly saw that the wound wasn't the only one along the creature's body. The length of the monster was covered in these circular marks. Most of them were about a metre in diameter, many of them were smaller, but John noticed at least one that was much larger.

John remembered seeing similar marks before on the back of a whale he had been tracking for a few weeks off of the west coast of Canada. That whale had been lucky enough to survive a fight with a giant squid. Its calf had not been as lucky.

Tentacles, John thought. *But what could be big enough to make marks this big?*

John looked behind him into the deep unknown. The ocean suddenly felt a lot bigger to him and he felt a lot colder in these waters. There was so much left to explore. He couldn't even see this creature's tail. His scientific mind longed for the unknown to become known, but as John swam in the water, looking out towards the hazy depths of the sea, he thought it would be best if this unknown remained unknown.

After John and Lawrence folded up their suits, and packed their gear away into the car, John slotted his camera's memory card into his laptop. The photos took a minute to load up, but when they did, he opened them all at once. He skipped past the photos of the basking shark he had taken with his students. That felt like a lifetime ago now. It felt like someone *else's* memory and not one of his own. He opened the last picture he had taken: the one of Lawrence surrounded by the tentacle marks.

'That's it, right?' Lawrence asked. 'Whatever left those marks must have killed it, don't you think?'

'You'd think so,' John said.

'But you don't?' Lawrence asked. Neither of them took their eyes away from the photo. They couldn't look away.

'I don't,' John said. 'I'm not sure. The wounds just don't look deep enough to kill a creature of that size. But whatever made these marks must have given it one hell of a fright. If it didn't kill it outright, this thing might have been scared to death.'

The words of Wallace Burns abruptly came to mind.

It's awake...

THIRTEEN

The second sign shall be the plants.
From an ancient Hebridean prophecy.

Ben and Alice Walters lived on one of the many farms on the south side of St. Budoc's Island. On the island, the main animals farmed were sheep and chickens – for their meat, eggs, and wool – but there was a dairy farm that supplied the island with fresh milk, too. Any beef eaten on the island had to be shipped to the island as part of the weekly cargo haul, so it was notoriously expensive. Fish, on the other hand, were plentiful and cheap. Most people had fish four or five nights a week – or at least they did until the fish washed up on the shore and fell from the sky. Suddenly, everyone seemed to lose their appetite for fish.

The Walters had bought their farmhouse but had sold their farmland to a sheep farmer who had rented the land from the farm's previous owner. The house was a two-storey stone-built house with a tiled roof. Short stone walls surrounded the house, dividing their homeland from the farmland.

John Calvary walked up the cobblestone path to their house with a bag over his shoulder containing his laptop. He wanted to show Ben the photos of the tentacle marks on the creature's side to see what he made of them. He noticed that Wallace had addressed Ben directly before John had tackled Wallace in the pub, and he was hoping that Ben might be able to shed some light on the photos. Ben was close with Mitchell Miller and seemed to be friends with other people of authority on the island as well. John had gotten the impression that Ben's circle of friends knew everything of importance that happened on St. Budoc's, and also had a certain level of influence over the island's affairs.

John reached for the heavy iron knocker on the Walters' front door and let it fall against the door with a loud thud. A few seconds later, Alice Walters answered the door. She was a pretty woman in her forties with dusty-blonde hair, light freckles, and pearl earrings. Standing behind her, holding onto Alice's leg, was young Penny Walters, Ben and Alice's five-year old daughter. She wore a pair of pink pyjamas and clutched a stuffed seal as she stared up at John with brown doe-eyes.

Alice opened the door with a neutral expression on her face, as if she wasn't surprised at all to see John there.

'Is Ben in?' John asked Alice.

'I'll get him,' Alice said and walked away without any pleasantries, leaving Penny behind. Penny raised the seal to cover her mouth, as if to provide all the protection and reassurance she needed to keep standing in front of the stranger at their front door.

'What's your name?' John asked her.

'Penny,' she replied. Her voice was muffled by the toy.

'How old are you, Penny?' John asked.

Penny held her hand out in front of her, showing her five fingers and said, 'This many.' Then she piped up, lowered her seal from in front of her face, and asked, 'Did you see the fish fall from the sky?'

'I did,' John said. 'It was scary, wasn't it?'

Penny shook her head then said, 'Nuh-uh. Not to me.'

Before John could reply, Ben walked into the entrance way from the living room to greet him.

'Penny, can you go and help Mummy?'

Penny ran into the house, carrying her seal with her. Behind her, John caught a glimpse inside their living room. There were a group of people sitting inside. He could see Mitchell Miller and a man he thought was the island's doctor, Dr. George Geiger. He was in his fifties and had snow-white hair. John also caught sight of the huge, round belly of another man, but couldn't see his face.

'It's nice to meet you!' John called after Penny as she disappeared into the living room. No one in the living room even tried to look at John. He looked back to Ben. Heavy bags sat beneath his eyes.

I guess he hasn't slept either, John thought, suppressing the urge to yawn.

'Can I talk to you for a minute?' John asked.

'Sure,' Ben said. He stepped outside and partially closed the front door so it rested on the latch without locking shut. Apparently, he didn't want John peering in.

'How's Wallace?' John asked.

'He's in a cell at the station,' Ben said. 'But he won't be properly seen to until we take care of that thing on the beach.'

'Why not?' John asked.

'We don't have the resources to escort him to the mainland,' Ben said. 'Someone would have to come and pick him up, and we just don't want any outsiders nosing into our business until we understand what that thing is. Present company excluded, of course.'

John didn't know how to take the fact that Ben just referred to him as a nosey outsider. He knew that the islanders didn't want him there, but he thought that at least Ben was happy to have him back.

'And Angus?' John asked.

'Jesus, John,' Ben said, looking back into the house to make sure no one could hear. 'He's only been dead a minute,' he said quietly. 'I haven't spoken to his family. That's not my responsibility, that's for Mitchell to do. I'm guessing there'll be a funeral sometime next week but, again, a coffin will need to be shipped to the island and we just don't want anyone knowing what we're dealing with at the moment.' Ben glanced back at the door, looking impatient.

'Is that why you came to see me?'

'It's actually about something Wallace said,' John told him. 'What do you think he meant when he said, "It's awake."?'

John noticed Ben narrow his eyes and quickly glance around John's face.

He's trying to suss me out, John thought. *Does he not think he can trust me?*

'He didn't mean anything by it,' Ben said. He was trying to look more relaxed, but the tightness of his stance gave him away.

What does he know? John thought. *Or, more importantly, what doesn't he want me to know?*

'But—'

'He's crazy,' Ben interrupted. 'You saw him yourself. Nothing he said made sense.'

'Something spooked him.'

'Everyone's spooked,' Ben said. 'First the monster, then the fish... It's actually a miracle no one else has gone insane.'

Haven't they? John thought as he remembered Victor Walters scaring Sarah and him on the night that he arrived. They weren't exactly the actions of a sane person, were they?

'How's your examination going?' Ben asked, glancing at John's bag. 'Have you found anything yet?'

'No,' John said. He clutched his bag closer to him. Maybe he shouldn't show Ben the photos just yet. If Ben was keeping something from him, John didn't feel as if he could be completely open with Ben, either. 'Not yet. Do you think Wallace thought that the creature was still alive? Do you think that's why he said—'

'Come on, John,' Ben said. 'You're venturing into the realm of conspiracy theories. The creature isn't anything more than a previously unknown species. You and I both know that. It's scary, sure, but there isn't anything more to it. I'm sure it was just as scary when humans first discovered sharks. Wallace has always had a screw loose, and after seeing that creature it finally fell out.'

John wasn't convinced. Ben's tone was casual, but his shoulders were tense. He was hiding something.

It's awake.

Ben let out a sigh. 'John, look. It's great to see you again. Really, it is. But I think it would be best if you just went back to…' He thought for a second and then asked, 'Where are you living at the moment?'

'St. Andrews,' John told him.

'I hear it's lovely there,' Ben said, nodding. 'I'd love to visit you there one day, but I think that right now you should go back. I'll arrange a boat for you in the—'

'I'm not going back,' John said. 'Not yet.'

'Just let us sort it out,' Ben said. He was struggling to hide his agitation. 'We'll be fine. Really. Thank you for your help, but we can take it from here.'

'I'm not leaving,' John said, and turned to walked away. He made it halfway down the path before Ben called out after him.

'That isn't a good idea, John. At least *think* about it!'

Sarah Calvary filled up a floral teapot with cold water from the tap. She had bought it from the second-hand shop a few doors down from her newsagents. Apart from books and clothes, the second-hand shop sold the belongings of the recently deceased. Families would bring any of their relative's furniture, crockery, and knick-knacks to the shop that they either didn't want or didn't think they could sell themselves. The shop was always busiest the week after a funeral, which was precisely when Sarah had bought this lovely little teapot, right after Agatha Mary Burns, Wallace's grandmother, had died. The shop was operated by the local church, and most of the proceeds went to the church to help pay Reverend Argyle's salary. The rest of the proceeds were donated to whatever charities the church congregation wanted to support.

Sarah poured the water from the teapot into the pot of a dying orchid. The pot was waterlogged from where she'd been overwatering it, trying to revive it. Over the past few days the blossoms had been dropping off and the leaves had started to yellow from the tips inwards. Only one blossom remained, but she wasn't willing to part with the orchid yet. Deep down she knew that the plant was already dead, but Claire had given it to her for her birthday last year and Sarah wasn't ready to let it go.

'Come on, you can make it,' Sarah said to the flower.

'It definitely looks past its best,' John said, looking up from his bowl of porridge. He had topped it with a knob of butter and a healthy sprinkling of brown sugar and walnuts.

'It was fine last week,' Sarah said. She poured the rest of the water from the teapot into the sink and rinsed it and then rested it, upside down, on the draining rack. She turned toward John, drying her hands on a dish towel. 'I was thinking about maybe going to church this morning,' she said. She was being somewhat coy in her statement, hoping that John would hear it as an invitation.

'When did you start going to church?' John asked. He hadn't caught on.

'They were so helpful when Mum and Dad died,' she said. 'After their funeral I just kept going and it started to make sense to me in a way it never had before.' She looked at John for a second, realised that he wasn't going to follow up with her, and then said to him, 'Come with me. We can go together.'

John laughed, almost choking on a mouthful of porridge, before realising that she was being serious. He leant forward in his chair and said, 'Oh. I don't know. I'm pretty sure they don't want people like me there.'

'It'll… It'll be fine,' Sarah said, with a flutter of uncertainty in her voice. 'We don't have to stay for long. Seriously. Once we're there, if you feel uncomfortable and want to leave, we can.'

John sighed. He could see that Sarah was being earnest and knew it would mean a lot to her if he went. 'I guess I'll have to change,' John said as he finished his porridge.

He put on his tweed suit and wore it with the nicest shirt he had with him. He took a dust cloth from under the sink and used it to wipe down his brogues, which had accumulated some mud around the soles.

What am I doing? John thought. *Going to church…*

He was ready before Sarah was. Sarah had put on a long wool dress and brushed her hair, which she clipped with their mum's old mother-of-pearl butterfly-clip, and even put on a little lipstick. It took years off her appearance and John thought she looked pretty.

John opened the front door. 'Sarah?' he said as he looked outside the house. His face dropped.

Sarah looked over to him as she put on her shoes. 'What is it?'

'It isn't just your orchid,' John said, pointing to the trees across the road. It was the end of spring. The trees had only just sprouted their leaves, yet outside it looked like autumn. The leaves on the trees were either dying or dead. Overnight they had gone from a luscious green to a light brown colour and had started to fall.

Sarah looked over at the trees. The grass beneath them was pale and wilting. 'The whole island is dying…' she said beneath her breath.

St. Budoc's Church was a quaint stone-built church that sat atop a rocky outcrop, looking out to sea. It was windy up there. A cornerstone had been engraved with the year that the church was built: 1638. The church had a red-slate roof and a short bell tower, whose bells could be heard over the entire island as they called in their congregation.

Inside, there was a large stained-glass window depicting Princess Azenor of Brest, holding a newborn Saint Budoc as she sat in a wooden cask, floating in the Irish Sea. The legend went that Saint Budoc was born in that cask after Princess Azenor fled France during a war of succession. The stained-glass was elegant and colourful. It was a nice contrast to the dark, brutish stone that the church was built out of.

About fifty people sat in the mainly empty pews, which were made from a hard wood. A woman in her sixties was softly playing hymns on a piano. John felt uncomfortable as he shuffled along one of the pews and sat down. The stares from the people at The Mariner's Dog were nothing compared to those of the congregation of the church, or at least that's how it felt to John. Sarah sat down next to him, clutching her Bible in her hands. She had bought it almost new from the charity shop but it had now become well-thumbed and dog-eared. John could see that her newfound faith had become an important part of her life.

The reverend was Robert Argyle. He was in his sixties and John assumed that it was his wife who was playing the piano. He was dressed in a grey suit that was slightly too baggy in the trousers and slightly too broad along his shoulders. He was the younger brother of Michael Argyle, the previous owner of Wallace's distillery. Michael had pursued his whisky, whilst Robert had pursued his Christ. After the hymns, the prayers, and the notices (which included the deaths of Claire Burns and Angus Brown but no mention of the cause of death), the pastor delivered his sermon.

'Isaiah twenty-seven verse one says, "In that day the Lord with his sore and great and strong sword shall punish leviathan the piercing serpent, even leviathan that crooked serpent; and he shall slay the dragon that is in the sea."'

He looked up at his congregation to gather their response, and then he addressed them directly. 'What we've seen this week is the work of God, slaying the dragon of the sea. And then when we look in the book of Job...'

He flicked through his Bible to find the bookmarked passage. 'Yes, when we look in the book of Job, chapter forty-one, again in the very first verse God says – and he's saying this to Job – he says, "Canst thou draw out leviathan with a hook? Or his tongue with a cord which thou lettest down?"'

He shut the Bible in his hands. Its reverb echoed through the church.

'No, we cannot,' Robert said. He let it sink in. 'But God, in his infinite wisdom and with incomprehensible strength, can. There have been a lot of strange things happening recently, and I know many of us are scared, but it says here...' he held up his Bible with both hands, '...it says here that God *slayed* the dragon of the sea.' He raised his voice when he said '*slayed*,' letting the word drag out a little longer. 'He *slaaayed* the dragon of the sea. God's in control. And if God is for us, then what could *possibly* be against us?'

He paused to let that sink in as well, looking over his congregation, hoping that they grasped what he was saying but he had made the mistake of pausing for too long. He had opened a gap.

An old woman, who John thought was at least in her eighties, with stark white hair and a thick, white knitted jumper to match, piped up and said, 'What about the fish that fell from the sky? Is that a sign from God too?'

Without giving the priest a chance to answer, an elderly gentleman also shouted out, 'And what about Angus and Claire? And Wallace? Is that God too? Has he deserted us?'

Robert Argyle's otherwise quiet, respectful congregation murmured amongst themselves as they took it in turns to call out. He stepped back from the microphone. He wasn't used to this kind of response. His sermons had only ever been one-sided before. He'd speak and they'd listen. They hadn't taught him this in seminary.

His congregation were unsettled and afraid. They were coming to him with questions that he wasn't able to answer, and as a result they were rising against him.

'What do you think?' Sarah asked in the car on the way home. John was sat in the passenger seat beside her, being rather quiet. She glanced over at him, but it wasn't long enough for her to figure out what he was thinking. Her windscreen was still cracked, which made it hard for her to look away for too long, for fear that she'd miss something in the road and hit it. She looked back at the road and lowered her head slightly to get a better look through an uncracked part of the glass. The other side of the windscreen had a new crack on it, which John thought had probably been caused by a falling fish.

John looked over at Sarah and said, 'I think there's something bigger going on here than fairy tales.' He regretted saying it as soon as the words had left his lips. He could immediately tell that Sarah was hurt by it. 'I'm sorry, Sarah, I just—'

'Last week you would have said that dragons were nothing but fairy tales,' she said, cutting him off. She paused, glancing at John. 'But here we are. And if they're real, then don't you think that maybe God's real too?' She pressed her foot down on the accelerator and didn't say another word until they were home.

FOURTEEN

Her blood shall anoint the earth.
From an ancient Hebridean prophecy.

'She looks bigger than she did on Saturday,' Lawrence said.

John and Lawrence were standing on West Beach, dressed in their wetsuits, looking at the sea monster lying on the beach. Its body was bloated.

'Are we assuming it's a "she" now?' John asked. He looked over at the creature. 'Its stomach is filling up with gas,' he said, not waiting for an answer. 'Last summer I was called to take a look at three sperm whales that had washed up on the beach in Skegness but unfortunately they called me in too late. By the time I was able to get there – it was nearly a seven-hour drive, by the way – two of them had already exploded.'

'That must have smelled nice,' Lawrence said, smiling.

John laughed. 'It smelled as nice as you'd expect. The guests staying at the Butlin's nearby weren't thrilled by it. We're going to have to let the gas out, otherwise it's going to explode. Cleaning up the guts of two sperm whales was no pleasant feat. This creature's the size of ten or twelve sperm whales, from what we can see at least. We still haven't located its tail. I'd hate to see this thing blow.'

'Me too,' Lawrence said.

'We'll need to reach its stomach to let the gas out,' John continued. 'Which, unlucky for us, seems to be about twelve metres below the surface over there.' He pointed about a hundred metres out to sea, where the body was well submerged beneath the waves.

Lawrence had been able to borrow a small, beat-up motorboat from the dad of one of his friends. John sat at the back and steered them alongside the creature until it disappeared into the sea. He cut the engine and the boat slowed to a stop.

Lawrence scooted over to the side of the boat and entered the water, falling in backwards and holding his mask against his face. He disappeared underwater for a second and then bobbed back up to the surface. He trod water as John pulled his mask over his eyes, attached his knife to his belt, and joined Lawrence in the water.

As John fell backwards into the sea, the chill of the water hit him instantly. It felt like skin was being ripped from his body. It took a minute for his wetsuit to get to work and warm him up. Finally, when it felt like he could breathe again, he looked over to Lawrence. 'Ready?' he asked.

'Ready,' Lawrence said.

They popped their mouthpieces in, took a few breaths of oxygen, and then submerged themselves in the water.

The visibility wasn't as good today as it was on Saturday. It was down to about nine metres. They couldn't see the bottom of the sea when they started to descend, and there was a brief moment where it felt like they couldn't see the surface anymore, either. John felt like he was completely closed in by the water. It was eerie.

They dived deeper, keeping a few metres away from the creature. After swimming for a couple of minutes, a giant fin came into view. John hadn't seen the creature's fins before. They were long. John imagined that they fanned out wide when the creature swam– they would have to, to propel such a large beast through the water. The edges of the fin were punctuated with needle sharp spikes, each about four feet long. They stretched out over part of the bloated stomach, which was trying to rise to the surface but was kept underwater by the sheer weight of the creature.

Why does it need such defences? John thought, and then he remembered the tentacle marks. He looked further out into the dark waters and quickly shook the thought away. Before returning to St. Budoc's Island, John wouldn't have said that he scared easily, but every little detail about the *leviathan* in front of him terrified him.

John paused and turned to Lawrence, pointing at the spikes to warn him of their presence. Lawrence saw them and made the 'OK' sign in acknowledgement. He kept his distance as they descended.

They swam towards the bloated stomach. The stomach was extended and had ballooned out, like a giant, misshapen rugby ball, and some of the creature's scales had peeled away from the skin as they stretched out.

John ran his hand over the skin, feeling the cracks in the scales. He knocked hard against the side of the bloated stomach and could feel the hollow vibrations under his hand. Some of the smaller scales that were peeling away were half a centimetre thick. It was its own personal armour, and yet it wasn't enough to protect it from whatever attack it had endured.

John was satisfied with the location. He unsheathed his knife, gently pressed it between two peeling scales, and began to score the skin with the blade, opening it up little by little. The creature had incredibly thick skin. Over the next ten minutes John worked his way through it, running the blade over and over the skin to deepen the cut until, finally, he had made it all the way through. In total, the cut was about a metre long and at least a foot deep. Once John had broken through the skin and into its stomach, a few bubbles emerged and raced to the surface. Then they started to pour out in a fine stream.

Good, he thought.

He gave Lawrence the 'OK' sign. Lawrence gave it back in return. It was a success. It would take several hours, maybe a couple of days, but the stomach would eventually expel all the pent-up gas that had built up inside, deflating the creature, and preventing a messy explosion on the beach.

John looked back and the bubbles started to pour out faster and faster. It was starting to look like someone had turned on a Jacuzzi. John could feel the water tremor around him as the gas shot out. It was uncomfortably warm.

Something's wrong, John thought. His skin prickled and he felt his mouth sweat, like the early warning signs of vomit.

He looked over at Lawrence through the cloud of bubbles. Lawrence spotted the concern in John's eyes, through his mask.

'OK?' Lawrence signed. He looked concerned now too.

John held out his hand flat and rocked it side-to-side, *'Something's wrong,'* he signed. He pointed his thumb to the surface, *'Go up. End the dive.'*

It was too late.

The stomach exploded.

A huge jet of hot air burst from the stomach and sent John flying underwater, spinning uncontrollably. The water around him quickly turned red with blood and he couldn't see anything. John couldn't tell if he was going up or down. His ears popped and then they popped again. Whichever direction he was going in, he was going there fast. His mask dislodged from his face and immediately filled up with the bloody seawater, stinging his eyes. His mouthpiece was knocked out of his mouth and trailed behind him like a loose water hose.

Panicking, he reached behind him for his mouthpiece. He found it and fitted it back into his mouth. As he did, his mouth filled with putrid water that was now full of gas and body fluids. It tasted of decay. John had to urge himself not to vomit. He pressed the button on his mouthpiece to expel the water with a blast of air and took in a deep breath of oxygen. He held out his arms and tried to kick to slow down his spiralling. He didn't want to kick too hard for fear that he was heading too deep underwater. All he could see around him were creamy-red bubbles and nothing else. Pain roared in his eyes. They stung like hell.

Then something soft bumped into him. He couldn't tell what it was, but thought it was probably a chunk of the creature's flesh. Then another one hit him.

On the water's surface, a volcanic spray of the creature's body parts exploded into the sky. It was like Mount Vesuvius erupting over Pompeii. It could be seen from almost everywhere on the island.

Reverend Robert Argyle saw the spray from his church, where he was busy working on next week's sermon. He looked up from his study Bible and looked out of the small window in his office to see what looked like wine erupting out of a whale's blowhole.

Alice Walters was driving to pick Penny up from nursery when chunks of flesh smashed down into her car. A moment later the road was covered with blood and patches of skin. She lost control of her car and skidded off the road, crashing into the grassy verge. Her front right headlight smashed and her airbags burst in front of her. For a second all she saw was white. That night she'd tell her husband how she thought she had died and caught a glimpse of heaven.

David Hedge, a man employed by the council to keep the streets tidy, was still cleaning up the fish that had rained down onto the high street outside of the Mariner's Dog. Mitchell Miller was sat inside the pub, which had been closed ever since Angus had been killed. He had cordoned it off with police tape but had helped himself to a small glass of ale as he ate his lunch: a ham sandwich and a bag of salt and vinegar crisps that he had bought from Sarah's shop. As Mitchell was eating his lunch, he was watching David pick up the fish and cast them to the side of the road. He heard the explosion, which sounded more like someone crashing into a bathtub, and then saw the blood rain down from above.

David looked up as he felt something soft hit his head, worried that it may have been from a passing bird. Instead, he saw blood, and it began to rain. Flesh fell like hail. A chunk of skin slapped Dave in the face. He yelled in shock and, not knowing that it was locked, ran straight into the pub's front door and smacked his head.

Mitchell shot up and quickly unlocked the door to let David seek shelter inside the pub. The two men stood in the doorway as David rubbed his head, watching the brief downpour of blood wash down the high street. It reeked of decay.

As the bubbles cleared, John searched for the light. Even though the visibility was poor, the surface was significantly brighter than the sea floor. He moved his head around, comparing the darkest parts of his vision to the lightest parts. The lightest part appeared to be behind him. He eventually righted himself and steadied his breathing. He looked down into darkness and up towards the light, which had now gone from a murky green to a dark shade of pink.

He tilted the top of his mask, pulling it away from his face, and blew as hard as he could out of his nose. The air expelled the majority of the water out of his mask. He did it a second time to expel the rest. The inside of his mask now looked somewhat hazy. The glass on the inside had been smeared by the fat that exploded out of the creature's stomach.

John had taken more SCUBA courses than he could remember – he even taught one the summer before he started his PhD – but none of them had prepared him for anything like this. He had stopped spiralling, but his body still surged with adrenaline and his heart beat rapidly. He slowly breathed in and out as he tried to lower his heart rate. He counted as he breathed in and counted as he breathed out. It was a trick Sarah had taught him. He couldn't remember the numbers that Sarah had said to count to, so he just counted until he couldn't breathe in any more oxygen, and then counted again until there was nothing left to breathe out. He needed to find Lawrence and make sure he was okay, but he couldn't do that if he was panicking.

After a few seconds John managed to regulate his breathing and he felt the pounding in his chest subside. John looked around him, trying to relocate the creature. The water was now full of blood and flesh, and the visibility had been reduced to only a couple of metres, but through the murk John saw a slightly darker patch of water and swam towards it. As he got close, the shape of the creature emerged from the water once again, but this time its stomach had been ripped open. Strings of intestines snaked towards the surface, reaching out of the chasm like pale, skeletal fingers.

Lawrence, where are you? John asked himself. He could feel the panic rising in his chest and looked around for any sign of Lawrence. John's ears popped again and suddenly he heard a muffled scream coming from his left. He swam as fast as he could until he saw the shape of Lawrence in the murky water.

As Lawrence came into focus amongst the floating debris, John saw that he had been thrown against the monster's fin. One of its spikes pierced through Lawrence's back and protruded two feet outside the front of his stomach. Lawrence's mask had been completely knocked off. His mouthpiece was floating by his side as he screamed and clawed at the spike, trying to get it out of him, but in his panic, he was pulling it the wrong way. He thought he was pulling it out of the front of his stomach, not realising that he was actually impaling himself even further onto the spike. John stared at Lawrence in horror as bubbles…

…gushed out of Patrick's mouth as he screamed. Someone was on top of him, forcing his face into the water, trying to drown him. His face was sideways, with his mouth and left eye completely submerged, but his right eye was above the water, staring at John for help.

John lay frozen beside him, not really seeing what was happening. He was in a drugged daze and couldn't focus on the image before him. Was he awake or asleep? What was *happening? He could hear Patrick scream. That's all he could really understand.*

His eyes slowly focused and he saw Patrick's bloodshot eye open in abject terror. But John couldn't recognise it as terror. He couldn't recognise anything in this nightmare. He cast his gaze around him and didn't know where he was, but wherever it was, it was old. It was really old. Strange religious symbols were carved into the walls along with text that he couldn't make out. Patrick's gargled screams seemed to drift farther and farther away.

John squeezed his eyes shut and then opened them wide, trying to force himself to be awake. It always worked in his dreams, and this had to be a dream. It had *to be.*

Then the shapes of the three men standing over Patrick came into focus. Who were they?

He looked to the other side of the room and could see down a long, faintly lit corridor. An ancient stone staircase led up to a small wooden door in a wall at the top.

John could feel himself starting to regain consciousness as if he were coming up to the surface from underwater. He gathered what little strength he had. He took a deep breath and stood up on shaking legs. His feet were unsteady and the room twisted around him. He spun with the room, keeping his eyes set on the door at the top of the stairs, and ran.

John's bare feet beat against the wet stone as he ran as fast as he could down the corridor. His mind felt like it was slipping in and out of consciousness. Everything was slow and fluid, and he couldn't get a sense of how fast he was moving. He caught a glimpse of the wall, and noticed that it wasn't just full of strange carvings and writing, but was covered in nightmarish images too. He looked up to the door. He didn't know if the men standing over Patrick were coming after him, but he didn't care. The door was his focus. He had to get out.

It was like running in a dream. Everything was slow and fluid. He couldn't get a sense of how fast he was moving.

John clambered up the stairs to the door. He climbed them using his hands and feet like a child. He didn't know how tall the staircase was, but to him it felt like he was climbing a pyramid. His hands and feet slipped on the wet stones as he climbed and he fell against the hard corner of a step. The pain shot through his chest as he finally reached the top and fell through the door, crashing onto the floor behind it. He looked up. He was in a temple, but not one he'd ever seen before. It was as good as ruins. Plants and creepers painted the walls and the crumbling pews. The roof was full of holes, letting God's rays pour in, and there was a giant gaping hole, where the door should have been.

John ran for it, clumsily at first, but he eventually found his feet.

He heard footsteps pounding up the stairs behind him, echoing through the long stone corridor, but he made it out of the temple before anyone could see him leave. He looked over his shoulder at the ruins of the temple behind him, which looked out over the sea like a hellish lighthouse over the River Styx.

He turned away from the temple and ran as furiously as he could, wheezing like an asthmatic. His head finally began to clear, and John realised that he wasn't dreaming, which meant that Patrick really was down there in the stone room beneath the ruins. Guilt and fear crashed over him. He couldn't leave Patrick behind, John thought as he continued to run away. He had to go back for him. John's mind thought one thing but his body did another. He kept running to save himself, even if that meant that Patrick...

…was dead. John snapped back to reality and looked at Lawrence, but Lawrence's eyes stared blankly into the distance. Wisps of blood floated from the wound in his stomach and strings of white beaded vomit hung suspended in the water as they floated from his mouth. Lawrence had died and John hadn't done a single thing to save him.

John carried Lawrence's limp body up the stairs from the beach and ran through the car park, screaming for help. He screamed so violently that it felt like his throat had been ripped out.

Tabitha Levin heard his screams and ran out from her fish bar, wiping her hands on the white apron she wore over her clothes. She saw John carrying Lawrence, limp in his arms, and raced over to them.

'What happened?' she shouted. She pushed her hair back as the wind blew it in her face.

John placed Lawrence on the floor of the car park and turned away, retching.

He wiped his mouth with the sleeve of his wetsuit and pressed the heels of his palms into his eyes until he saw stars. He couldn't look at Lawrence again. The image that had been haunting his nightmares ever since that night thirty years ago – the image he thought of every night and had to shake from his mind every morning when he woke up – now lay before him on the pavement.

Not again, John thought. *Not again. I can't lose him again.* He began to weep.

Tabi dropped down beside Lawrence and checked his pulse, and then looked down and saw the hole in his stomach through his wetsuit. It was four inches in diameter and she could see the asphalt through him. Tabi checked his breathing, but she knew it was useless. He had stopped breathing long ago.

A waitress in her thirties opened the door to Tabi's Fish Bar and shouted after her, 'Tabi?'

Tabi turned around and shouted back, 'Call Dr. Geiger!'

The waitress rushed back inside and the door slammed shut.

'It's too late,' John said. He walked in circles, keeping his back to the body. 'It's too late.'

FIFTEEN

A father grants permission but a mother grants forgiveness.
An old Hebridean proverb.

John lay in his childhood bed. The wooden bed frame hurt as it dug into the back of his ankles. His sore eyes stared lifelessly up at the ceiling. The textures and patterns swirled and formed shapes in front of him, as they did on countless nights when he was a child. First, he saw the boat, then he found the fish, then the textured ceiling rearranged its patterns into a screaming face.

His mind flashed between Lawrence, dead in the water, and Patrick, drowning in the temple. Both of their faces haunted him. He'd spent endless nights focusing on Patrick's face so that he wouldn't forget him after he had left the island. The first thing he always remembered were his eyebrows. They'd always stood out to him. Then he thought of the shape of his jaw, before finally thinking about his lips, pressed into the ground as he drowned.

You could have saved him, John thought. In his healthy mind he knew that was a lie, but now, as his body clenched with anguish, it felt like it was the only thing that was true. *You could have saved them both.*

He should have rescued Patrick. He should have fought off whoever those men were. Had he seen them on the island since coming back? Did they know that John had returned? They must have. They knew who he was back then, and chances were they were still alive. Unlike Patrick. He should have carried him, like he carried Lawrence, and rescued him from that god-forsaken temple.

But what temple? John thought. That was the only time he had ever seen it. The island wasn't terribly big, and he had travelled every inch of it on his bicycle as a teenager, but he had never seen a place that matched the images in his hazy memories. *Somewhere high, so you can see the sea.*

The question had gnawed at him for years, and he had looked out for the temple as he arrived at St. Budoc's in Callum's boat. He had scoured the tops of the cliffs, looking for anything that resembled a temple, but by that time the mist had already thickened. It must have been on the other side of the island.

I should have rescued him, John thought as he remembered the barbed fin piercing through Lawrence's stomach. He remembered the agony in his eyes as he unknowingly pulled himself further onto the spike. John should have pulled him free. He should have shared his oxygen with Lawrence as they ascended to the surface. He should have lifted him into the boat. He should have applied pressure to the wound and given him mouth-to-mouth. He should have kept Lawrence alive so that when Dr. Geiger finally arrived he could have saved him. He should have gone with him in the air ambulance to Western Isles Hospital. He should have sat with him as he recovered. He should have been by his side when he finally awoke from his coma. He wanted to do for Lawrence what he could never have done for Patrick.

Instead, he had let him die. Lawrence was dead.

I'm responsible for both of their deaths, John thought.

There was a gentle tap at the door. John didn't acknowledge it, but Sarah came in anyway. She pushed the door open with her back as she held a tray of tea in both hands. The same teapot she used to water the orchid was sat on the tray along with a plate of lavender shortbread.

'I brought you some tea,' Sarah said. She set it down on the bedside table next to John, pushing away a book on marine ecologies that John had been planning to study for next semester's syllabus. He had only touched it once since returning to St. Budoc's.

'Can I sit down?' Sarah asked as she perched herself on the edge of the bed. There was barely enough room for John, but she managed to find space for herself to sit down, half on, half off the bed. The calming aroma of the bergamot in the Earl Grey tea rose with the steam and filled the room.

'I never should have come back,' John muttered.

'You couldn't have foreseen this,' Sarah said. 'No one could have.'

'I *should* have, though,' John said. 'This is my job. I could have helped him. If I had acted quickly... but I froze. This whole place is cursed. I don't know why you want to stay here.'

'It's my *home*,' Sarah said. She brushed a stray curl of hair behind her ear.

'You have no family here,' John said.

That cut Sarah deeply. She looked away from her brother and said, 'I had you...'

'But I couldn't stay, and you know that,' John said. He kept his eyes on the ceiling, speaking slowly and dryly, like he was on his therapist's couch. 'I've spent the last thirty years trying both to *remember* what happened to Patrick and trying to *forget*. But nothing makes sense. Someone must have told on us – they couldn't handle a couple of teenagers in love and just leave us alone... I had to run.'

'I'm sorry, John,' Sarah said and clutched his hand. Her hands were soft and dry. He found them comforting. 'That never should have happened. You were both so young, and scared, and experiencing something new and exciting. But you didn't have to cut me out of your life. I was scared too, John. I heard that you and Patrick were involved in an accident and—'

'He was murdered,' John said and let go of Sarah's hand. 'There was no accident.'

'But we didn't know that then,' Sarah said, edging towards him. 'We were told that you were in an accident. We searched the whole island looking for you. We didn't realise you'd left. We didn't hear from you for a year. For a *year,* John. You didn't even leave me a note. I spent that year thinking you were dead, but praying every day that you were still alive.' She dabbed her sleeve to her eyes to dry away the tears. 'Then when we found out you were alive... did you not even think about how we would have felt? Maybe if you had stayed you could have spoken to the police, and they would have found out who had killed—'

'Don't,' John said. He shuffled his body until he was sitting upright with his back against the headboard. 'Don't you dare put this on me.' John felt the guilt that had been gnawing at him flare up into a roar in the pit of his stomach. He didn't need Sarah to make him feel worse than he already did.

'What?'

'I know I should have told you. *I know that.* And I'm sorry for putting you – and Mum and Dad – through that, but I had no choice. If you knew where I was, who's to say they wouldn't have gone after you too, trying to find me?'

There was a knock at the front door.

'Drink your tea,' Sarah said. 'You'll feel better.' She stood up and plucked a tissue out of the box next to John. She wiped away the tears beneath her eyes as she left the room.

John stared up at the ceiling as he listened to Sarah walking down the stairs. There were three more knocks at the door. They were louder this time, and sounded angry. Sarah's steps sped up as she trotted down the stairs. John heard the front door click open and then the voice of Mitchell Miller.

'Where is he?' Mitchell asked in a growl. All pretence of friendliness was now gone.

John's heart skipped a beat and he sat forward. He put his feet on the floor, listening. Mitchell wasn't alone. John could hear the angry voices of a host of others behind him.

John stood up and walked downstairs. He didn't have to guess why they were here. They were here because of Lawrence.

Sarah saw John out of the corner of her eye as he descended the stairs and looked up at him with fear in her eyes. Behind her was a mob of about fifteen people and Mitchell Miller was front and centre. Ben Walters stood just behind him, ashamed to make eye contact with John and Sarah and looking generally uncomfortable.

Mitchell locked eyes with John. He pointed his finger at him and, with a voice like gravel, said, 'You *murdered* him.'

'Sarah,' John said, as he put himself between her and Mitchell. 'Will you go into the living room.' It wasn't a question. It was a command. He wasn't going to have her caught up in this.

Sarah stepped back to give John space but she stayed right there with her feet planted firmly to the ground as if to claim her territory. She wasn't going anywhere. John had often seen his sister as someone he needed to protect, but then he remembered that when Victor Walters harassed them the other day, Sarah was the one that grabbed the knife from the kitchen and protected him.

'You *knew* that thing was going to blow and you let Lawrence carry on anyway,' Mitchell said. 'You let him die.' His chest heaved with every word.

'I'm sorry,' John said. 'I really am, but we had no idea what was going to happen. We tried to let out the gas slowly but—'

'*You blew it up!*' someone shouted at the back of the mob. John couldn't see who it was but Mitchell knew straight away. He turned around and stared daggers at them. He was in charge, everyone else was just there to back him up.

Mitchell then signalled to two guys who John didn't recognise. They were big, but only a few years younger than Mitchell and himself. He must have known them from school, or at least had seen them when he was at school, but now they were just strangers from the mob. They barged past John, purposefully knocking him with their shoulders, and then marched upstairs.

'Hey!' Sarah shouted after them. She reached toward them, trying to pull them back, but John grabbed her wrist and pulled her towards him.

'It's okay,' he said so that only she could hear him. He looked into her eyes so she could see that everything was going to be fine. When she understood, he let go of her wrist. Sarah moved back to where she was standing. She rubbed her wrist where John had held her.

'Hannah, come here,' Mitchell said. He turned to a middle-aged woman next to him, grabbed her by the shoulders, and forced her to stand in front of John. She wore black trousers and a yellow knitted jumper. Her hair was dark black with strands of silver shining through. She shuffled uncomfortably, not knowing where to look. Her arms were folded in front of her.

'Mitchell, please don't…' Hannah said, pleading.

Mitchell ignored her. 'Look into her eyes,' he said to John. 'Tell her why you let her son die.'

It's Hannah Miller, John thought. *Mitchell's sister-in-law… Lawrence's mum…*

Hannah averted her eyes. Her whole body was rigid and there were tears brimming her lower eyelids. She couldn't stand to look at John.

'Mitchell, please…' Hannah said, straining her neck to look away from John.

'Come on, Mitchell,' John said. 'Mrs. Miller. I'm sorry about what happened. I really am. We had no idea what was going to happen. Lawrence was a good—'

'Don't start with that crap,' Mitchell interrupted him.

'Look,' John said. 'If you want me to explain what happened, I will. I'll tell you everything: what our thought process was, what we were trying to find… but I can't tell you like this. There's nothing I can say that will satisfy you when you've come to me with an angry mob. If you really want to hear what happened, let's arrange a time tomorrow and I'll explain everything. Then you'll see that it was an accident– a *tragic* accident that no one could have predicted.'

Mitchell's eyes narrowed. He lowered his voice and said, 'Why did you come back here? Was Patrick not enough? You had to take one more?' John's stomach dropped. Mitchell eyed John up and down in disgust. 'You were probably too busy checking out Lawrence's arse to—'

Fury raged through John's blood. His anger rose from his stomach, through his chest, and into his head. He grabbed hold of Mitchell's shirt and yanked him forward, knocking him into Hannah as he did. She let out a startled yelp as she stopped herself from falling. Mitchell's eyes widened in fear. John had caught him off guard.

'If you had let me bring a *team* over it wouldn't have just been me and *Lawrence*,' John said, spitting out every word an inch from Mitchell's face. 'But for some goddamn reason you and the rest of the inbred vermin on this disgusting rock are too up your own arses to ask anyone else for help.'

Mitchell quickly glanced at John's hands on his shirt. Despite looking frightened he spoke coolly. 'Careful what you do next, John,' he said. 'Assaulting an officer will land you six months behind bars... maybe more.' He nodded to the mob behind him. 'And I've got about fifteen witnesses who will testify against you, no matter what I choose to accuse you of. That being said, prison might suit you, huh?' He raised his eyebrows.

Ben stepped forward, out of the crowd. 'I think he gets the point,' he said as he separated them, sliding his hands between them and gently pushing them apart.

John relaxed his hands. They were stiff and sweaty. He clenched them a few times to loosen up his fingers and to keep his blood flowing.

'We're all upset about what happened,' Ben said to John, taking his hands away. 'I know it isn't explicitly your fault, but not everyone understands that,' he said, looking at Mitchell. 'It was great to see you again, it really was, but look around you... we have a lot to take care of here. Things have changed since you were last here. Don't you think it's best that you leave?' The crowd behind him murmured their agreement. 'Please John, we need time to mourn in private. You can go home now.' He said it as though he were giving John the permission to leave, but there was a note in his voice that made it sound more like a warning.

'This is the biggest scientific discovery of our lifetimes,' John said.

'And you think that's something worth dying for?' It was the first time Hannah had addressed John himself.

'Hannah is right, John,' Ben said. 'We can take care of it from here,' One of the men that had gone into the house came back downstairs with John's camera in his hands. 'Thank you,' Ben said to him and took the camera. He turned it on and started going through the photos John had taken.

'What are you doing?' John said and tried to snatch it from him, 'Give that back.' But Ben pulled the camera away from him and continued to look through the photos, stopping on a group photo of John's students before their dive.

'We don't need anyone else following you here,' Ben said. He continued flipping through the photos until he reached a photo of the creature and stopped to inspect it. He smiled, satisfied that this was the memory card he needed. He went through a few more photos and stopped on the one of Lawrence's hand inside the tentacle mark. Ben's brow furrowed. He quickly ejected the memory card before anyone else could see it and dropped it into his pocket.

'Why are you doing this?' John asked. He was worried enough that Ben was taking his memory card and hoped that Ben thought that was all the evidence he had. He didn't want to let on about the spearhead, or – God forbid – all the photos he had backed up onto his laptop.

'I feel like you haven't been totally honest with us,' Ben said. 'I've arranged for a boat to take you back to the mainland tomorrow morning. You'll be back home before you know it.'

Panic struck Sarah's face. She looked desperately at John.

'And if I don't go?' John asked.

Ben signalled to the mob behind him. Fifteen angry men and women – and Hannah Miller, who looked empty and frail beyond her years – stared at John.

'Well, we might just have fifteen witnesses who saw you assault a police officer,' Ben said and smirked.

Suddenly, any feeling of warmth John had toward Ben turned sour in his stomach.

'You bastard.'

'So what do you say, John? Will you go?' Ben asked. He smiled, revealing a set of perfectly white teeth. He may have been Patrick's brother, but Ben's smile was ugly as sin. Why couldn't Ben have been the one to die, leaving John to live the rest of his life with Patrick by his side?

'Gladly,' John said.

'John, you can't,' Sarah said, stepping forward. 'Ben, please don't make him leave.'

'It's for the best,' Ben said. 'But you can visit him as soon as we sort out our business on the island.' He glanced up at the stairs as the second man came down carrying John's laptop. He snatched the laptop from the man's hands.

'Give that back,' John said, but the man ripped it away from him.

That was it. All of the photos John had were on the card in Ben's pocket and backed up onto his laptop. He didn't have any other evidence, apart from the Viking spearhead that he had hidden away.

'The boat leaves from the port at eight in the morning,' Ben said. 'We'll give you your computer back then. It'll feel brand new. Wiped clean. A blank slate.'

'I have all my work on there,' John said. 'Please, don't do this.'

'Oh, I'm sure you have a backup in your office,' Ben said, and then looked at Sarah. 'Are you okay taking him in the morning or do we need to arrange a police escort?'

'I'll take him,' Sarah said. She swallowed, as though she was trying to dislodge something stuck in her throat.

'Good,' Ben nodded and smiled sweetly at her. 'It'll give you a chance to say goodbye. I'm sorry it ended up like this, John. I really am. But maybe we'll see you again in another thirty years.' He handed John his now-empty camera and left.

SIXTEEN

Their wings shall close so your eyes may open.
From an ancient Hebridean prophecy.

The house was quiet. John lay in bed, looking out at the almost full moon and the whispers of clouds passing in front of it. He held the Viking spearhead in his hand, turning it over, letting it catch the moonlight and reveal the intricate carvings. The moon was bright and filled his room with a pale blue light. The spearhead cast a long, sharp shadow across the floor.

The spearhead was the last piece of evidence he had left, and John had spent the evening studying it, hoping it would hold enough information to help him unravel the mystery of the creature but by this point, he was invested in more than just the creature itself– he wanted to uncover the connection between the creature and the dying island. Yes, the beached monster was a scientific marvel, and if it had washed up anywhere else, dozens, if not hundreds, of people would have been called in to study it, but for some reason the people on this island would not reach out to the mainland for help, and John wanted to know why. He had a feeling that it was for a reason bigger than just 'keeping it in the family.' Something else was going on here, something that they were hiding.

How long had you been buried in its flesh? John thought. The spearhead felt cool and heavy in his palm.

He imagined a long Viking boat sailing over the frigid sea. He could see its sail, blooming in the wind, and a hundred oars rowing in unison. The ship wouldn't have sailed so much as glided across the water as it followed a long black shape that moved like slick oil beneath the waves. The eager Vikings would have watched from their boat, tracking the shape, their helmets low over their faces and their capes billowing behind them. John could imagine one of the Vikings raising his spear in anticipation, ready to launch it at any second at the monster hiding beneath the waves.

John got out of bed and dressed himself. He hadn't wanted to return to St. Budoc's Island, but the place had beckoned him back and trapped him. Since the moment Sarah picked him up at the dock, he had hated every second he'd spent there, yet instead of fighting for his freedom, John felt compelled to stay. The creature on the beach had him under its spell and he couldn't leave now. In a similar way to how the Vikings had hunted the creature with ships and spears, John was also on the hunt. He needed to know more.

John finished tying his shoes and walked across his old bedroom as lightly as he could so that he wouldn't alert Sarah, who he hoped was sound asleep. He crept down the stairs, skipping the few steps he remembered that creaked and landing instead on a few that had started to creak in his absence.

He grabbed Sarah's car keys out of a bowl on top of the radiator by the door and made his way outside to her car in the pale moonlight. He got in and shut the car door as quietly as he could, wincing as he turned the key in the ignition. If Sarah wasn't completely asleep she would have heard him start the engine but, just in case, he kept the lights off as he drove away from the house so they wouldn't shine into her bedroom. John strained his eyes to see in front of him. The cracks in the car's windscreen made it hard to see in the daytime, but in the light of the moon it was almost impossible. He kept the lights off for the first couple of minutes and only turned them on after a few minutes when he was sure he wouldn't be seen. It didn't help the visibility by much, but it helped a little. John slowly drove across the island, all the way to West Beach.

When he got to the beach, he parked his car a few spots down from where Lawrence had parked that morning. The moon felt brighter on the beach. The sky had completely cleared, revealing the waxing gibbous in the night sky. It hovered only a little way above the horizon, letting its reflection ripple in the waves beneath it.

John walked along the beach. His shadow, elongated by the midnight moon, reminded him of Dracula's shadow in an old movie he'd seen. John's was long and thin and looked like it had a life of its own as it skittered across the uneven sand. John made his way towards the creature. Despite its stomach being so far away, the smell of its exploded carcass was almost unbearable. All sorts of alien-looking entrails floated in the water and the beach was covered in chunks of flesh that were waiting for the high tide to carry them out to sea. Most of the larger, heavier chunks from the explosion had landed near the creature. The chunks became smaller the further away they were from the creature. The smell was unbearable.

The sea itself was a deep, silky black, its calm surface in stark contrast to the carnage on the beach. Small pockets of mist had begun to form way out near the horizon, blurring the line between sea and sky in several places. John glanced out towards a part of the horizon that was still uncloaked by the mist. There was nothing but open water for a thousand miles between him, on the West Beach of St. Budoc's Island, and Newfoundland, on the east coast of Canada.

John thought of the vast expanse of water before him, and of its unimaginable depths. *What else lurks in these waters?* he thought. His mind jumped to the giant squid the Newfoundland fishermen had encountered. *They must have been terrified.* There was enough room between St. Budoc's and Newfoundland for all kinds of monstrous creatures to hide in the depths of the sea, just waiting to be discovered or to wash ashore of some lowly island and terrorise the islanders.

John approached the creature's head. He raised his camera and took a photograph. Mitchell Miller had taken the memory card John had used during his dives with Lawrence, but he hadn't found John's spare. John liked to keep one memory card in a different bag, just in case something happened. It didn't have anything on it, he had wiped it clean before he left for the trip with his students, but that was why he had come out tonight. If he was going to be leaving the island, he was taking evidence with him. The camera flash illuminated the monster, catching some of its iridescence. Deep greens, blues, and purples rippled along the creature's skin and were gone in an instant. As the flash disappeared, and John's eyes adjusted back to the darkness, he looked at the creature's hollow eyes reflecting the stars as it stared off into eternity.

What are you? John thought. *Where did you come from? Why are you here?*

As he looked into its eyes, he sensed a feeling of greatness. Of majesty. He felt almost as if he was in the presence of something that was all-knowing. John moved around the creature and its eyes caught the reflection of the moon, making it look alive.

It's awake...

But John knew for a fact that it was dead. It couldn't be anything *but* dead. Especially with its stomach ripped open, and its guts sprayed out halfway across the island. Even if by some chance it had been alive before it had exploded, it couldn't possibly still be alive.

Right?

John took his knife out of his bag and cut away a small part of the creature's flesh below one of its many eyes.

I'm not leaving empty handed, he thought. He'd be able to analyse it back at work and discuss it with his colleagues and eventually they would be able to figure out what type of animal it was. John needed to know.

He dropped the flesh into a small, plastic, zip-lock sandwich bag and it squelched as it hit the plastic. He zipped up the bag and dropped it into another zip-lock before putting it into his shoulder bag. He didn't want the sample to leak, and he didn't want anyone to be able to smell it and confiscate it.

As he zipped up his bag, John was startled by a loud splash out at sea. Although the splash sounded far away, it was so loud that it sounded as though a car had been dropped into the water. He stood still, his heart thumping, and looked out over the ocean, trying to see what had made the noise, but the water near the shore was black. About a mile away from him, a large ripple spread across the surface. As the waves rippled out, they caught the moonlight and shattered its reflection into a million little pieces.

Sarah's orchid was now completely dead. The leaves were dry and yellow and the water in the pot was almost overflowing, yet Sarah watered it anyway, trying her best to salvage the plant. The orchid was a gift from Claire, and it was the first one Sarah had ever owned. With her friend now gone, Sarah couldn't bear the thought of the orchid dying too.

Sarah had laid out a small, but thoughtful, breakfast on the kitchen table. There was a carton of orange juice, a plate of toast, and some scrambled eggs made with an extra knob of butter, a generous shake of salt, and a sprinkle of dried tarragon. Sarah didn't cook very often, but that morning she wanted to keep her mind occupied. She turned to the sink to empty out the tap water from the teapot and dropped in two English breakfast tea bags ('Why do they have to call it *English* breakfast,' her dad would always say), and filled the pot with boiling water from the kettle.

She heard John come down the stairs and looked up. He had one bag over his shoulder and was dragging his suitcase behind him, thumping as it hit every step on the way down. She watched John walk into the kitchen and flicked her eyes from his bags to his face. She smiled at him in a way she hoped was reassuring.

'Hungry?' she asked.

John saw the spread laid out on the table and felt touched at the effort Sarah had put into it. He saw that she'd even put down a clean tablecloth and he recognised it instantly. It was the same tablecloth his mum had used for their Sunday roast the Sunday before he had run away. 'Famished,' John said and smiled. He sat down and buttered some toast, adding eggs on top for himself and Sarah as she poured them each a cup of tea.

'I've been thinking,' Sarah said.

'Yeah?' John asked.

'I think I'm going to come with you,' she said. 'To St. Andrews... if I won't be a burden, that is.'

'That's wonderful!' John said. He wasn't sad to leave the island, but he was sad to be leaving Sarah. Knowing that she was planning to come with him made all the difference. 'What made you change your mind?'

'You,' she said. 'This place is home but, *"there's no stronger connection than family."* That's how the old proverb goes, isn't it? Anyway, I won't come straight away. I'll need to close the shop and sell the house...' she looked around the kitchen and her eyes misted over with memories of the place– of all the Christmases and birthdays spent around this very table, '...but it'll be worth leaving to have my brother again... to be a sister again...'

'Thank you,' John said, reaching out to squeeze his sister's hand. 'It's been nice being a brother again. Hopefully I can be a better one from now on.'

They finished their breakfast, and at seven-thirty John put on his shoes to leave.

This is it, he thought. *I'm heading home.*

Yesterday he had been anxious about leaving without the materials he needed to study the creature, but now that he had a piece of the creature and the photographs he had taken last night, he could examine them all back in the safety of his own office. The photos he had now were nowhere near as good or as detailed as the ones Ben had stolen from his camera, but they were all he had. He would need to remember to back the new photos up as soon as he got his laptop back from Ben, or whoever Ben had given it to, to wipe clean.

Sarah picked up her car keys from the bowl atop the wooden radiator cover and opened the front door. As she stepped outside, she slapped her hand to her mouth and yelped.

'Sarah?' John got up and stepped past her to see what had startled her.

On the road in front of Sarah's house lay about twenty dead sparrows. Each one had splattered against the ground. Some of them had broken necks. Some of them had exploded on impact and their tiny organs spilled out like worms that had shrivelled in the sun.

John looked at the sparrows and then looked up at the sky and realised that there wasn't a bird in sight. He then noticed that there wasn't a single birdsong in the air, either. Normally the island was alive with the sounds of the birds: geese honking as they flew overhead, pigeons cooing as they nested in trees, and curlews wailing on the beach as they hunted for shellfish. This morning, however, it was perfectly still.

The whole island is dying, John thought. *Ever since that creature washed up on West Beach the island has been falling apart. Had the monster been keeping the island alive?*

As Sarah drove John to the harbour, they both stared out the windows at the groups of birds that lay dead around them. Most of them were gathered in flocks, with broken bones and burst bodies, as though they had simply dropped out of the sky mid-flight. John kept raising his eyes to the sky, hoping to see a pigeon, or a crow, or even a gull, but there was nothing. It soon became apparent that there wasn't a single living bird left on the island.

'They're everywhere,' John said as they passed another flock of sparrows. He did eventually see a seagull, but it wasn't alive. Its body was nothing but skin and bone, lying on top of a stone wall. One of its wings had snapped in half upon impact. It must have hit the wall with quite a force. It was crawling with ants.

'I don't like this, John…' Sarah said. She looked out of the window at the wilted flowers and yellow grass. Most of the plants were dead now too. 'I don't like this at all…'

As they continued down the road they came out into a clearing and for a moment John caught a flash of something dark and grey atop of a hill in the distance. His heart lurched into his mouth.

'Stop!' he yelled.

Sarah jumped and slammed her foot on the brakes. 'What is it?' she asked. She looked ahead of her, thinking that there was an animal or another car or something that she was about to crash into.

'Go back,' John said, looking over his shoulder. 'Reverse!'

Sarah looked bewildered, but put the car in reverse and backed down the road. John leant over her to look out of the driver's side window until the small grey blur came into sight from behind an autumnal tree at the edge of the road.

'There! Stop!'

Sarah stopped the car. She put it in neutral and pulled up the handbrake.

John strained his eyes, trying to make out what it was. It was a long way off, but he could just make out the shape of a small grey-stone structure that looked like it was in ruins. John felt his skin tense and a chill sprung goosebumps along his neck. He knew exactly what this was. John was looking at…

…the temple through dazed eyes. He couldn't keep them open. He felt his body bounce up and down. Someone was carrying him. Who? His eyes were heavy with sleep. He tried to force his eyes open, but only managed to open them a crack. The temple bobbed up and down in front of him. Another shape was moving beside him. He forced his eyes to open wider. He could just about see Patrick being carried in the arms of a tall, thin man. Who are they? Patrick's head lolled up and down. He was limp in the man's arms. John tried to keep his eyes open but couldn't. They were too heavy. Before he finally closed them, it dawned on him that they were both being carried towards…

…the temple. John couldn't believe that he had found it. He yanked his seatbelt away from him, opened the car door, and leapt out.

'John?' Sarah called.

'I'll meet you back at home,' John shouted over his shoulder as he ran away from the car and towards the ruins of the temple.

'What about the boat?' Sarah shouted.

'Go home!' John yelled.

Sarah watched as John ran away from her. For a moment she didn't know what she was supposed to do. She eventually put the car in gear and turned it around. John knew what he was doing and she had to trust him.

John approached the temple and saw that it was perched near the edge of the cliff. Ocean waves crashed into the walls below, making this one of the few places on the island that smelled of the sea and not of the creature's rotting flesh. The grass around the temple was tall and brown. As the wind blew in from over the sea, the dead grass whispered.

The temple itself was built out of grey stone, like most of the buildings on St. Budoc's Island. It was well weathered. Moss clung to the north side of the temple, and dying ivy clung to the walls, as if begging for its life. The roof had almost completely collapsed in on itself. It was a miracle that the temple was still standing at all. John couldn't tell how old the temple was, just that it was very old. However, despite the age of the temple, the front doors were new. They were tall and dark and the paint on them hadn't even cracked yet. There was a part of the ivy that had obviously been hacked back to allow for their installation.

John slowed down as he approached the temple. *These aren't ruins. People still come here,* John thought. *They still use this place.*

John looked around. Satisfied that no one had followed him and that he was all alone, he pushed the doors open. They were unlocked and opened without a creak.

Inside, the main room of the temple was as dilapidated as the outside. The remains of disused pews were scattered throughout. Over the years they had broken and rotted away and someone had cleared them out of the way to open up the floor of the temple. John wondered if whoever had moved them didn't want to dispose of the pews on the island for fear of raising suspicion. Curious islanders would ask where the pews had come from and confess that they didn't know there was another church on the island.

How many people know of this place? John thought. He'd never heard anyone talk of it before. Not a single person. He only knew it existed because he had been brought here with Patrick, but that had felt like a dream. He didn't remember telling Sarah about this place. He wasn't even sure he had told his therapist. Until this moment, it had lived alone in his mind.

At the front of the temple was a crumbling altar. It had been built out of the same grey stones as the rest of the temple and stood high above the pews. Behind it stood a large stained-glass window. Many of the panes of coloured glass had broken and laid on the floor beneath it, but John could just about make out what the window was supposed to depict. It was a giant fish swallowing a man.

Jonah? John thought. That would have been the logical answer, but as he looked at the window, something about the image struck him as odd. John moved closer to the window as light shone behind it, illuminating the glass. The fish that was swallowing the man – the person John assumed was Jonah – had the same spider-like eyes as the creature lying on the beach. It had one large fish eye at the front with four smaller black eyes trailing behind.

They know, he thought. *They've known what it is all along.*

A gentle murmur of voices rose from within the temple. John turned around to see if someone else was there, but he was alone. The temple was empty. He looked past the front doors, expecting to see someone, but the space was as empty as it was when he arrived.

The voices were faint, and John couldn't make out what they were saying. He listened. They seemed to be coming from the opposite end of the temple. John slowly walked towards them, careful not to make a sound. If he was able to hear them, then whoever was speaking would be able to hear him too.

At the far end of the temple John could just barely see a door beneath a tangle of dead ivy. It didn't look like anything other than a cupboard, but it was the only other door John could see. He pushed it open, and it opened onto a tall stone staircase. As soon as he saw it John was struck with an image of his hands and feet on the cold stone of the steps. His stomach tightened as his muscles tensed and his hands began to shake. He stepped backwards. He felt as though there was an invisible barrier before him, preventing him from entering. He just about remembered running up them on his hands and feet after he had escaped...

...and left Patrick to die...

...but he couldn't remember it clearly. It was a picture, not a movie.

The murmuring was clearer now. It sounded like a group of men, but he couldn't be sure. The fear in John's stomach rose into his throat and his knees began to tremble. Every instinct was telling him to run in the opposite direction, but John knew that everything he was looking for lay at the bottom of those stairs.

The stairs descended into darkness. John went down one step at a time, with his right hand on the wall beside him. There wasn't a handrail on the other side and John wasn't sure how far down the drop was, but based on how cold the air had turned, and how distant the voices still felt, he didn't think he'd survive a fall. The stairs were slightly slippery, and John wondered if they were covered in moss. It was like walking on rocks at the beach.

As John ran his hand down the wall, he felt water drip from his fingers. He made his way down the steps in darkness, but eventually, he reached the bottom of the stairs where he could see the faint glow of light at the far end of a long cave-like tunnel. The voices were louder now, and John crept towards the light, edging further down the tunnel. The tunnel felt strange, yet sickeningly familiar. It was all starting to come back to him. He remembered running down this very tunnel as he escaped and felt fatigued just thinking of it.

As he walked closer to the light, he could start to make out the carvings on the wall. They must have stretched the entire length of the tunnel but it was only now that there was enough light for him to see them. There were ancient patterns and symbols that he didn't recognise, and a series of tableaux that had been carved into the rocks. One of them depicted an ancient ship.

A Viking ship? John thought, and wondered if the carvings were made by the Vikings themselves. Could the temple have been built by Viking settlers? John wasn't sure if Vikings had a history of using stained glass, but he knew that they had visited the Hebrides after the invention of stained glass. The architecture and design of the temple was vastly different to that of the tunnel, and the carvings in the wall were a different style to the scene depicted in the stained glass. John wondered if whoever had built the temple had done so because that's where its builders had found the entrance to the tunnel.

John looked closer and saw that the carved ship was engulfed by giant tentacles that stretched out from the water as it dragged the ship and its sailors down into the water, into the monster's domain.

What is this? John asked himself. He never had found the creature's tail. Could it have tentacles instead of the serpent-like tail he had imagined? Or was this monster something else entirely?

As he continued to walk down the tunnel, he saw writing etched into the walls, alongside the images. It was in an old, weathered script, but it was in English. He strained his eyes to read a part of it in the dim light. It said, *The waters shall reveal their age.*

Reveal their age? John thought. *What does that mean?*

The tunnel opened into a small grotto inside a larger cave, but the light that John was following looked like it was coming into the cavern from outside. The cave must have opened onto the beach below. John carefully stuck his head around the stone wall of the tunnel and could hear the wind and the waves. If there were any birds left on the island, he might have heard them too.

John edged his way into the cave, inching closer to the voices, whilst staying hidden against the cave wall. He took his pocket knife out of his trousers and opened the blade to use it as a mirror. He was careful not to let it catch the light in case it reflected it across the room and gave him away.

John got as close to the voices as he dared and slowly moved his knife around until he could see a group of people standing together in the grotto, talking amongst themselves. He counted. There were thirteen people in total. He recognised Ben Walters, Mitchell Miller, and Dr. Geiger instantly but he wasn't sure about anyone else. Some he could see but didn't recognise, and others had their backs to him so he couldn't see their faces.

Behind them was a wide opening in the cave that led to a secluded beach outside. By their feet, in the floor of the cavern, were shallow pools of water that had filled up with seawater when the tide had come in. John had seen those pools before, and despite the haziness of the memory, he knew that this was the place that had haunted him for years. A mixture of sorrow and rage boiled up inside him. The image of Patrick's bloodshot eye filled his memory and it took all of John's strength not to cry out. This was the place that John had left Patrick to die.

John felt faint as his blood turned icy with hatred. It was becoming progressively harder to control his breathing. He leant his head against the cool stone of the cave wall and used his sleeve to try to muffle his breathing as he took deep, silent breaths, forcing himself to calm down. He needed to remain hidden.

With shaking hands, he raised the pocketknife again and could see Ben Walters in a heated discussion with a tall, overweight man in his seventies. John could see his huge, curved belly, but couldn't see his face. He thought he recognised his voice, but he had no idea who it was.

He was at Ben's the other night, John remembered. *Maybe that's why I recognise him.*

'Did you learn nothing from your father, whilst he still held on to his sanity?' the man said to Ben. 'The island is dying. First the fish, then the whisky, now the birds… It's all carved into these damned walls. We know what's coming next. The prophecies make that very clear. How long before it'll be us who die?'

His voice… John remembered it from his childhood, hearing it echo down the corridors and leading morning assemblies at school, and it all came flooding back. He knew why he recognised him. He was his old headmaster…

…Mr. Sutherland, sat at his desk. Across from him were John and Patrick. Mr. Sutherland's belly pulled his shirt taught, like a hotel bed sheet stretched over an overstuffed mattress. He poured tea into a china cup and put it on the desk in front of Patrick. Then he poured another one and sat it down in front of John.

'There you go, boys,' Mr. Sutherland said. 'Drink up…'

John and Patrick looked at each other, unsure as to whether or not they were in trouble. Then John looked up as…

…Mr. Sutherland stared from Ben to Mitchell and back to Ben again. Then he said, 'We have to leave.'

'Leaving the island in the middle of all this is just foolish,' Mitchell said.

'Foolish?' Mr. Sutherland asked. His voice had aged since the last time John had heard him speak.

'I've worshipped Kaala my entire life,' Mitchell said. 'My father worshipped her before me and my grandfather before him. She has allowed us to *thrive* on St. Budoc's. Whilst the people from St. Kilda found it impossible to sustain themselves, causing them to turn from their way of life and return to the mainland, Kaala spared us the same fate. We have always been able to survive, and it was Kaala that has sustained us. Where is your faith? We knew this day was coming. The Prophet wrote about it. After she dies a new god will take her place.'

Ben joined in. 'Wallace was right. It's awake.'

'And therefore, we have to leave,' Mr. Sutherland repeated. 'Kaala blessed us abundantly, but this won't be our god. We don't know what it is or whether it will bring blessings or curses.'

Ben nodded and turned to the rest of the group. 'He's right,' he said. 'Just look at what it's already doing to our island. It's killing it.'

'It's a hard restart,' Mitchell said. 'That's all. The island is preparing itself for the new god. It'll be reborn. *We'll* be reborn. In a few months it'll be like nothing had ever happened. This new god will lead us to paradise.'

'I'm starting to think that Wallace had the right idea,' Ben said.

'To shoot his wife?' Mr. Sutherland asked.

'No,' Ben said, correcting himself. Then he paused, thought for a second and corrected himself again, 'Well, actually… yes. Maybe death is the right choice here. This island has pledged allegiance to Kaala for as long as it's been occupied. We can't just give that up and worship another god, if it even *is* a god.'

'That'd be unfaithful,' another man, who John didn't recognise, agreed.

'Death *would* stop us from having to make that choice,' Mr. Sutherland said.

'But at what cost?' Mitchell asked. 'What if this was part of Kaala's plan all along? Wouldn't you rather see what was going to happen than duck out now?'

Dr. Geiger stood there, listening quietly as each person presented their case, and when he finally spoke, he did so with authority. 'There's one thing that's weighing heavy on my heart,' Dr. Geiger said.

'Dr. Geiger?' Mr Sutherland urged him to continue. Everyone quietened down and listened intently.

'The afterlife,' Dr. Geiger said, letting the word hang in the air as he turned from person to person. 'If these gods are real, which evidently they are, then so must be the afterlife that the Prophet so vaguely wrote of.'

'What's your concern?' Ben asked. 'That the Prophet wasn't explicit enough?'

'Kaala may have been faithful to us,' Dr. Geiger continued, 'but there's no saying that this new god, whoever he or she is, will be as faithful. For all we know, it may have been this new god that killed her. And if it did kill our god, what do you think it will do to us, her followers?'

John remembered the tentacle marks along the creature's back. Along *Kaala's* back. *That was her name, wasn't it? That's what they called her. That's who they worshiped.* John felt a sickening feeling rise up in his stomach. All he'd wanted since seeing the monster on the beach was answers, but now he felt like he'd heard too much. He didn't want to be listening to this. It was like accidentally hearing a couple argue, unaware that they were being too loud. It wasn't for his ears.

'The question isn't whether or not it will send us to Hell,' Dr. Geiger continued, 'but what kind of *Hell* it has dominion over. That's something that I don't want to ever find out. And it's something that I don't wish for any of you to find out either, dear brothers.'

John couldn't believe what he was hearing. A few days ago, he would have thought this conversation was all nonsense, but after everything he had seen on the island, he knew that there was a terrifying truth in what Dr. Geiger was saying.

Is there a Hell? John thought. *And does this god have control over it? Or is that just what these people believe? There are so many religions in the world that they can't all be right.* Not that John had ever believed that *any* of them were right. *But if there is one religion that got it right– that truly understands who God is– I pray that it isn't this one…*

As John listened, his knife slipped from his shaking fingers, and in a panic he shot his hand out to grab it. He hoped for the handle, but he would have settled for the blade. He missed, and watched it tumble through the air in what felt like slow-motion. The knife hit the stone ground and clattered, echoing all along the tunnel.

His heart lurched into his throat.

The thirteen people in the room stopped speaking.

John held his breath, but he was certain that even if they couldn't hear his breathing, they'd still be able to hear his pounding heart, pumping adrenaline through his veins. His temples throbbed in pain. He needed to breathe.

'Someone's here,' Ben whispered.

John crouched down carefully to pick up his knife, making sure not to let it make a single sound against the floor.

He was about to take a step forward but hesitated. His shoes would be too loud. He hastily untied them, picked them up, and ran.

He ran down the tunnel in his socks, into the darkness and towards the stone staircase. His feet slapped against the wet stone, and suddenly John was thrown back into his nightmare, stumbling through the dark corridor toward the door at the top of the stairs.

'John!' Ben shouted after him. His voice echoed throughout the tunnel and bounced back to him.

He tore after him. John didn't care that he could barely see where he was going. His body was so full of adrenaline that it felt as if his legs were running on their own. He could hear Ben's shoes beat against the ground behind him. Ben caught a brief look at John's leg just before he disappeared through the door at the top of the stairs.

John burst through the door and ran into the temple. He darted for the door.

Seconds later, Ben reached the top of the stairs, and as his head broke into the temple light, he saw the temple door slam shut. It reverberated throughout the stone structure.

'John!' he shouted after him.

John ran as fast as he could away from the temple. His inner thighs burned as they rubbed together. The road Sarah had driven on was too far away. If John had run for it, it would have taken him so long to get to that Ben would be able to see him and follow him. To his left, John saw a row of thick bushes. They had completely died but were thick enough that he couldn't see through them. He dived over them, burying himself amongst the leaves that hadn't yet fallen away, and tried hard to catch his breath without making a sound.

John watched, with his hand over his mouth and nose, as the temple door opened and Ben ran out. Ben was terribly out of breath. He paced forwards for a few steps and then stopped. He leaned forward with his hands on his knees and inhaled several sharp, deep breaths.

As far as Ben could see, no one was there.

John had disappeared.

SEVENTEEN

An act of love can shake the earth.
An old Hebridean proverb.

John hid behind the bush until he was certain that it was safe to leave. He had managed to calm down enough so that his breathing was quiet. Moments after Ben had come outside the temple, Mitchell and a few others had joined him, but after a few minutes of searching for John, they went back inside. John heard their voices inside the temple, followed by the sound of the door above the staircase being shut. He stayed behind the bush for another ten minutes, until he was absolutely certain that they were out of sight, and out of earshot.

His knees clicked as he stood up. His calves were burning from crouching for so long and the back of his hands had light red scratches from where the bush had grazed him as he jumped behind it.

John was still trying to process what he had heard in the tunnels.

The creature was a god, John thought. He had no idea how they could worship such a thing. He wondered if they had seen her before, swimming in the waters where she lived, or if they had worshipped her in blind faith, believing that she was real but never laying their own eyes upon her.

The temple was her *temple,* John thought. *What did they call her? Kaala? Was that it? And what about this new god they spoke about. Could the new god be whatever creature left those unholy tentacle marks along Kaala's body? Was the new god the tentacled creature depicted in the stained-glass window?*

John's mind raced with a million thoughts. He asked himself an endless stream of questions, but he couldn't answer a single one. There was one question in particular that stayed at the forefront of his mind.

What does this have to do with Patrick?

John hurried down the residential street on his way back to Sarah's, trying not to draw attention to himself. He tried to move quickly and remain hidden, as he suspected that there would soon be thirteen pairs of eyes – if not more – out looking for him. He didn't know who else on the island he could trust. Unfortunately, there wasn't any other way to Sarah's house than down this road and past all these houses. He looked over his shoulder to make sure no one was following him. There was no one behind him. Dead trees swayed in the breeze causing leaves to float to the ground as though it were autumn. Many of the houses had their curtains open but were too dark inside for John to see if anyone was peering out. John kept his head low and picked up his pace.

On either side of the street were small stone cottages. Some of them had the traditional thatched roof, now littered with dead birds and fish. The cottages sat in stark contrast to the modern cars in front of them, almost all of which had cracks in their windows or dents on their roofs or bonnets. Dead birds remained on a number of the cars. Others lay twisted on the ground where they had either fallen from the sky or bounced off a car roof.

A few houses down, John saw an older gentleman frantically loading bags into his car. He lifted suitcase after suitcase and crammed them into every available space. He was fitting one into the back seat of the car, when he noticed John and turned to look at him.

It was Victor Walters, Patrick's father.

The two men froze when they saw each other. Aside from Ben and Mitchell, Victor Walters was the last person John wanted to see right now.

Victor threw another bag into his car and then rushed over to John, scowling. His wrinkles accentuated his expression.

'What are you doing here? You're supposed to be on the boat!' Victor yelled, stumbling toward John. Spit flung from his mouth as he shouted. John wished he would keep his voice down.

'Believe me,' John said, stepping back, 'I'd rather be.'

'No, no…' Victor said, shaking his head and looking distressed. He turned around to look at his car full of his belongings and then back to John. 'This is bad. This is really bad.' Victor's wiry eyebrows, white with age but yellowed by smoke, trembled and his expression flashed between fury, anxiety, and fear.

'Mr. Walters, I know you blame me for Patrick's death,' John said. 'And that's something that I've had to live with for the last thirty years of my life. But something terrible is going on and—'

John stopped speaking when he saw Victor's face. His mouth hung open and his eyebrows stilled. He looked stunned. Hurt, even.

What did I say? John thought.

'You... You think I blame you for Patrick's death?' Victor asked. His voice was much quieter now, and quivered as he tried to hold back tears.

'You do...' John said. He was confused. 'Don't you?'

Victor shook his head, causing a small tear to fall on the ground. 'You were the best thing that ever happened to Patrick,' Victor said. John stared back at him in shock.

Victor's face was now streaming with tears. He wasn't trying to hold them back anymore. 'Patrick never came out to me. I've prayed to God that he would have, but prayer can't change the past. I think he was afraid of how I'd react... In those few weeks, though, he was the happiest he'd ever been since Martha passed, and I know that was because of *you*, John. *You* made him the happiest he'd ever been.'

Now it was John's turn to cry. He could feel his throat tighten and his eyes turn warm with the first warning signs of tears. He breathed in, trying to still his emotions.

'Then why were you threatening Sarah and me?' John asked. 'Why did you smash her windscreen and leave that note?'

'You're not safe here, John. This whole damned island is going insane,' Victor said as he waved his arms, gesturing to the houses around him. 'Something bad is happening. I can feel it... I think you can feel it too... I don't want you to be a part of it.'

John looked at Victor. The entire time he had been on St. Budoc's, he assumed Patrick's father was his enemy, but with all the new questions he had swimming around in his head, John needed a friend now more than ever. As he looked into the old man's tear-streaked face, he made the decision to trust him.

'I just came from the old temple,' John said.

Victor's eyes widened. 'You were there?' His voice was hushed. He looked around him to make sure no one else could hear them.

'I wasn't the only one,' John said. 'I overheard Ben and—'

Victor shushed him. 'Not here,' he said, looking over his shoulder. 'Come inside.' Victor took hold of John's elbow and ushered him into his home. It was the same house that Patrick and Ben used to live in. Victor led John into his living room, and John suddenly felt at peace. It was a completely different feeling from when he had stepped back into his old home. Maybe it was because a part of Patrick was still here, or maybe it was the homely smell of yesterday's soup that wafted out of the kitchen.

The Walters' home hadn't changed much. It had dark hardwood floors, which had seemed to darken even more with age, and peeling floral wallpaper. Despite living alone, and despite half of his family having died, Victor was a family man. Photos of his wife, Martha, and of his sons hung on the walls. There wasn't a surface that didn't have a happy face staring back at him. John stopped to look at Patrick's old school photo. His white teeth shone as he smiled.

He really had a beautiful smile, John thought, and remembered why Lawrence had reminded him so much of Patrick. John remembered the day they had taken that year's school photos. His mum had given him a new brush and a tub of pomade and watched as John styled his hair, so that they didn't have the same disaster as the previous year's photo when John had a huge cowlick that the photographer ignored. John was sure that Sarah would have kept his school photos. They were probably in a cupboard somewhere, filed away in a photo album. Seeing Patrick's photo made him want to find his own. At least he had some fond memories from his teenage years.

Victor poured a generous serving of whisky into a glass and offered it to John. 'Drink?'

'I wouldn't if I were you,' John said.

Victor frowned and took a sip. He immediately spat it back into the glass, trying to avoid spilling it on the carpet, and stared at the bottle standing on the table in horrified disbelief. It was like looking into a crystal ball that had just revealed his death.

'What the hell happened to the whisky?' Victor asked.

'It's what drove Wallace Burns insane,' John said. 'Even the water's starting to taste funny.' John sat down on the sofa. The padding was thinning and needed to be replaced.

'It really is the end of the world,' Victor muttered. 'Well... *our* world,' he added with a dry chuckle. He dropped the bottle into the bin and placed the glass in the kitchen sink.

John felt comfortable in the lounge, but he was eager to get back to their conversation. 'Did you know that they used to worship that...' he tried to think of the right word and then settled on, '...monster?'

'I did,' Victor said, lowering himself into his armchair with a grunt. 'I used to worship her too.'

'You're one of them?' All of a sudden John felt trapped, and he made a movement to stand up.

'God, no, sit down,' Victor said, dismissively. He waved his hand as though refusing a biscuit. 'I haven't for years.'

John was sceptical and kept his eyes on Victor as he sat back down onto the sofa, using his hand behind him as a guide. He wanted to trust Victor, but then again, he had also wanted to trust Ben.

Victor was a worshipper too? Did Patrick know about this? John thought.

Victor didn't say anything for a while. He just looked down at the floor, casting his mind back. John caught a brief quiver in Victor's lip. He took a deep breath and spoke.

'About a quarter of the island worship her,' Victor told him. 'They have done for centuries. I suspect that at least another quarter of the island are aware of some strange beliefs, and the other half of the island probably have no idea. Even your parents knew about it.'

'They worshipped it too?' John asked. He couldn't imagine his sweet parents being wrapped up in something so sinister.

'Heavens no,' Victor said. 'Sorry. Don't get me wrong, they didn't worship her, but they knew that people on the island worshipped *something*. I don't know what they thought of it, or if they even believed the rumours to be true. Your parents weren't the religious type, not unless it was Easter or Christmas, if I remember.'

'That's about right,' John said. 'At least twice a year they'd drag us to church for some holiday or another. I was never interested, but Sarah was. She goes to the church now,' John said, remembering the church service he went to with Sarah. 'So,' John continued, 'that creature's a god?'

'They seem to think so,' Victor said. 'We'd take her sacrifices and offerings. Beneath the temple there's a tunnel that leads to a hidden beach. It's surrounded by rocks, and the tunnel is the only way you can get there. We'd leave the offerings on the beach for the waves to claim them and deliver them to Kaala, and in exchange, she would provide us protection and plenty of fish. She was the reason our forefathers didn't starve to death when they first arrived here, or so we were told. Did you ever find out how she died?'

'I think so,' John said.

It's awake...

Victor leaned forward, eager to hear. 'How?' he asked.

'I think she died of fright,' John said.

'Fright?' Victor's wiry eyebrows jumped. 'What could possibly frighten a creature as big as—' He stopped as he suddenly realised. 'Oh,' he said and slowly leaned back into his chair. His face had turned white.

'There were huge tentacle marks along the creature's side,' John explained. 'But none were deep enough to kill it. I think she managed to get away before that happened... but I believe the shock was too much, and her heart just stopped.'

'It is awake, then,' Victor said under his breath. His eyes were filled with a quiet terror and darted around, unable to settle, as he tried to understand what this meant.

'The new god...' John said.

'You know?' Victor said, looking up.

'I overheard,' John told him.

'Let me finish loading my car,' Victor said, 'then we're getting the hell off this island.' He stood up and checked his watch. 'I'm leaving at noon. Get Sarah and meet me at the dock. If you're not there by then, I can't stick around. I should have left this island a long time ago. You had the right idea.'

'I didn't leave,' John said as he stood up. 'I escaped.'

'That was when I parted ways with the worshippers,' Victor said. 'I didn't want to be a part of the group that had my boy killed and tried to kill you.'

'I don't remember that night at all,' John said. 'Since coming back, little bits have been coming back to me... but for the most part I just can't remember any of it.'

'I don't suppose you would,' Victor said. 'They thought that because you and Patrick were...' he chose his words carefully, '...together, Kaala was punishing them. The fishermen were catching fewer and fewer fish, and half the cattle on the island caught some disease and had to be put down. They thought that if they sacrificed you to her, then she might bless them again...'

'They wanted to sacrifice us?' John asked. He couldn't believe it. How could anyone in their right mind think that they were being blessed by that creature, or that it would care or even know who he chose to love. The rage John felt at the temple returned and he felt sick again. 'Were you a part of it?' John asked.

'No!' Victor said, 'and I can't believe you'd think I'd ever hurt my boy. I was the one that tried to protect you both. When Ben told me about the two of you, I made him promise not to mention it to anyone. I feared what might happen if anyone found out. But he went to that bastard, your headmaster, David Sutherland, and—'

'It was *Ben*?' John's rage now completely flooded his body. *How could Ben have told on us? He was my friend. He was Patrick's brother.* Suddenly, John had to leave. He needed to confront Ben.

'Where are you going?' Victor called after him.

John didn't respond as he stormed towards the front door. His head was boiling. He opened the door and just before he slammed it shut he heard Victor shout after him.

'Just be at the boat by noon or else I'll have to—'

The rest of his sentence was lost after the door slammed behind him.

The god known as Kaala lay gutted on the beach, but her eyes – her many eyes – seemed to be staring all knowingly, as though she were still alive, as though she were still in control. Her face was still but something in the gleam of her cloudy eyes made it look as if she was relishing in the pain of the inhabitants of St. Budoc's Island. She rejoiced in it.

A low rumble shook the beach. The water vibrated and tiny grains of sand jumped up and down, a little at first, but then they leapt higher and higher. As the beach shook, the sand hissed like a giant snake hunting its prey.

The ground trembled and a crack formed along the beach, like a blade of lightning piercing the sand. The ground shook, then jerked apart and separated, leaving a foot-wide gap. Sand quickly poured into the crack, filling in the space that had just formed, hiding it from anyone who might have seen. The trembling stopped and the sand settled into the crack.

It was almost unnoticeable.

John pounded his fists against the front door to Ben's house. Earlier, he was trying to hide from Ben but now he was compelled to find him. He couldn't believe that it was Ben who had ratted him and Patrick out. All these years he assumed that it was probably Victor. He thought that Patrick's dad had hated him. But it wasn't Patrick's dad, it was Patrick's brother. *Ben.*

'Open up!' John shouted. He pounded on the door until he could hear movement on the other side. His fist throbbed in pain. 'Ben, you bastard, open the door!'

'Penny, get back,' he heard Alice shout inside. 'Go upstairs!'

'Mum?' Penny said.

'Upstairs!' Alice shouted. She waited a second and then unlocked the front door.

As soon as she had opened the door a fraction, John knocked it open the rest of the way and pushed right past Alice, shoving her against the wall and sending a framed photo crashing to the floor.

'Where is he?' John yelled. 'Where's Ben?'

Alice stood against the wall, stunned, and didn't answer. John stormed into the house. He looked in the kitchen. It was empty. He pushed open the door to the living room. There was nothing but toys scattered on the rug.

He came back to the entryway and looked up at the stairs.

'Ben!' he yelled.

He spotted Penny. She was sat on the stairs, peering through the gap in the bannisters, secretly watching what was happening, trying not to be seen.

'Where's daddy, Penny?' John asked, affecting as calm a voice as possible. He was trying not to scare her but, judging by the way she scampered away, he had scared her even more. 'Where is he?'

John tried to follow her upstairs, but instead he fell and hit the stairs hard. He jerked his hands out in front of him to protect his fall but landed painfully as his arms, chest and stomach all struck different corners of the steps beneath him. Alice had yanked his leg out from under him.

'Get out!' Alice shouted. John heard Penny slam her bedroom door shut upstairs.

John turned around to see Alice standing over him. Rage boiled in her eyes. She clutched a large kitchen knife in both hands, pointed right at John's face. Her stance widened and her face was tense. The muscles on her neck stiffened.

'Where's Ben?' John asked.

'You have five seconds to get out of my house,' Alice said through gritted teeth, trying to prevent Penny from hearing her, 'five seconds before I slit your *goddam* throat.'

John stood up. He held both hands out in front of him. 'I'm not going to hurt you,' John said, trying to remain calm. 'But you need to tell me where Ben is. Has he come home or is he still at the temple?'

'I don't need to tell you a goddamned thing,' Alice said.

John moved towards the door, keeping his eyes on Alice. Alice circled around the opposite way. They were like two boxers in the ring. She kept her eyes on John and her hands tight around the knife. Her knuckles had turned white.

'Do you know that your husband calls that creature his *god*?' John asked.

Alice didn't respond. She remained firm in her stance.

'Did you know that he had his own brother killed? He had him sacrificed to appease the wrath of a fish.'

Alice's grip tightened around the knife. Her arms straightened.

'Don't think for a second that if little Penny falls in love with a girl at school that he wouldn't do that same thing to her.'

Alice's face turned white with shocked fury, but John made a move for the door and left before she could reply, leaving the door wide open behind him. As soon as he had stepped over the threshold he heard Alice kick the front door shut, slamming it so hard that it shook the windows. If there were any birds left alive on the island they would have taken to the sky.

'Penny?' Alice shouted from inside.

John marched away from the house in the direction of the temple.

EIGHTEEN

With them the Seed of Wisdom did I sow,
And with my own hand labour'd it to grow:
And this was all the Harvest that I reap'd –
"I came like Water and like Wind I go."
XXX from The Rubayat of Omar Kahayam

Beth Rabbit was restocking the refrigerator with Irn-Bru, Coca-Cola and bottled water whilst Sarah was sat behind the counter, manning the till and doing some paperwork. She looked up as the bell above the door chimed and John walked into her shop.

'John,' she said and stood up.

'I need to borrow your car,' John said.

'Where did you go?' Sarah asked as she rummaged around her purse looking for her car keys. She pulled them out and handed them to John. He snatched them from her. 'I've been worried all morning, waiting for Mitchell or Ben or someone to come, wanting to know why you never got on the boat.'

Beth glanced over from the fridge. She was concerned. Sarah hadn't mentioned any of this to her.

'Did you know they worshipped that thing?' John asked.

'What?' Sarah asked.

'It's their god,' John said.

'Whose god?' Sarah asked.

'That's the reason they killed Patrick and tried to murder me. To appease it. They were going to sacrifice us to it. They *did* sacrifice Patrick to it, whatever the hell that means.'

'John, what are you talking about?' Sarah said. 'Who are you talking about? What is whose god?'

Beth had stopped to watch their exchange. She had one hand on a bottle of water in the fridge, and the other on the box of soda behind her. She looked at John, worried that he might be crazed, and glanced up at Sarah to see if she should be concerned.

'All these years I didn't understand what had happened,' John said. 'But now I know it's all because of some goddamn fish. And to top it all off, it was Ben!'

'What was Ben?' Sarah asked. She was struggling to follow John's chain of thought. 'You're not making sense, John.'

'He was the one that ratted us out,' John said. 'He told everyone about Patrick and me. If it weren't for him, Patrick would still be alive. He was supposed to be my friend!'

John turned to the front door.

'What does this have to do with my car? Where are you going?' Sarah asked.

'I'm going to see him,' John said.

'I don't think that's a good idea,' Sarah said, but the door slammed shut before she could finish.

John floored the accelerator and tore down the road in Sarah's car. The broken windscreen looked like a kaleidoscope as he tried to see the road through it. He was no longer trying to avoid the fish and birds that lay in the road, and instead he smashed their bodies into the pavement as he drove over them. The car shook so hard as he hit them that John didn't notice the ground shake beneath him.

Wallace Burns sat in his cell clawing at his naked body. His clothes were in a crumpled heap in the corner of the room. He tore deep, long scratches into his skin, covering himself in bloodied stripes. His nails had now broken and were jagged and caked in his own blood.

His jail cell was small and featured a hard plastic bed, which wasn't intended to be slept on for more than a single night, a toilet without a lid, and a small sink that was barely big enough to fit both hands in.

Half-way through a fresh scratch, Wallace felt the quake. His bed shook, the metal toilet bowl hummed like a wineglass being rubbed, and there was a sound like a passing freight-train coming from beneath his feet. He stopped and sat up. He searched every corner of the room with his eyes, trying to understand what was happening.

'What was that?' he asked the empty cell.

Panic flooded his face. He jumped off the bed and ran to the metal door, banging on it with both of his fists and leaving streaks of blood on the door with each hit. He leaned down to the small hatch used by the officers to pass him trays of food and shouted through it.

'Hello? What's going on? What was that?' he yelled but there was no answer. No one cared about Wallace Burns anymore.

John turned onto the road where he had left Sarah that morning. He reached the spot where he had left Sarah and turned to drive over the dead grass toward the temple. Once he was close, he slammed his foot on the brake and the car skidded in the grass, carving ruts into the mud. John opened the car door and ran into the temple, not bothering to close the door behind him.

'Ben!' he yelled. His voiced thundered against the stone walls of the temple. When John was in the temple earlier, he did all he could *not* to be heard, but this time he *wanted* to be heard. He wanted Ben to know he was there, coming for him. He was no longer afraid. He was furious. John shoved away the ivy covering the door at the back of the temple and hurried down the stone stairs as quickly as he could without slipping.

'I know you're here!' John shouted. His voice echoed down the tunnel before shouting back at him.

His feet pounded against the floor as he ran toward the light and into the cave at the end of the tunnel, where he had seen the thirteen worshipers have their private meeting earlier.

At the time, he hadn't been able to get a good glimpse of the room through the reflection in his knife, but now he could see it perfectly. He knew exactly where he was. This was the room where he and...

...Patrick was face down in a shallow pool of water. John looked over to him and saw his screaming face. His mouth was open, boiling the water with his screams. Around him was a crowd of people standing– watching. At first, they were a blur, but one by one he began to recognise them. The crowd that surrounded them...

...now hung from the ceiling of the cave. Ropes were tied around their necks, connected to long wooden beams that stretched across the ceiling. Nearly everyone John had seen that morning were now hanging like macabre Christmas ornaments from the roof of the cavern. Everyone except Mitchell Miller and Ben Walters.

Mitchell Miller stood atop a stepladder with a noose draped around his neck. Another noose hung empty beside him. Mitchell looked nervously at the corpses decorating the cave.

'Are you sure this is—' Mitchell began to say when he saw John walk up to them. Before he could finish his thought, Ben cut Mitchell's question off by kicking the stepladder out from under him. Mitchell's arms violently flung up towards his neck. It only took the second that he fell for John to see that Mitchell had changed his mind. Mitchell didn't want to die– his eyes made that very clear. If the fall had lasted a few extra seconds, Mitchell would have tried to pull the noose from his neck, but unfortunately, he was out of time. The rope pulled taut, and his neck cracked as the ladder clattered against the wet stone ground.

John winced at the sound. It echoed around the room and disappeared in the tunnel.

'You decided to come back,' Ben said, finally acknowledging John.

'You told them about Patrick and me,' John said, trying to stay calm despite what he had just seen.

Ben set the stepladder upright again. Mitchell's body swung between them on the end of his rope and the wooden beams above him creaked under the weight. Ben moved the ladder beneath the empty noose. This one was for him. John looked around at the other worshippers. They were all dead. Just like that, it had all come to an end.

'So now you know,' Ben said, matter-of-factly. He had little interest in John now. His mind was preoccupied.

'You had your own brother killed,' John said.

'It was the only thing I could do,' Ben told him. 'My Father was too much of a coward to do anything about it. Every day I heard people complaining about the lack of food on the island. The fishermen were catching fewer fish. The cows were producing less milk. I watched my Mum cry over the rising cost of imported food. My parents were worried that they'd have to move to the mainland. If I hadn't said something, we'd have all been punished.'

'She's not a god,' John said. 'You think she has this power, but she doesn't.' Then John corrected himself. 'She *didn't.*'

'But that's where you're wrong,' Ben said. 'After our offering, the fishermen caught record numbers of fish. That spring, the number of livestock born on the island doubled from the previous year.'

'Well then, if she's so powerful, how come she's dead?' John asked.

'She's being replaced. By what, I'm not quite sure, but I'm not sticking around to find out.' He climbed the stepladder and placed the noose around his own neck. He pulled the rope tight so it sat against his neck.

'You were willing to let your own brother die… for a fish?'

'Is that what your research told you? That she's a fish? Well I'm glad you were able to put your expertise to good use,' Ben said. 'Time well spent.' The noose was so tight against his throat that it moved up and down as he spoke. 'These gods are all over the world,' he continued. 'The Canaanites had *Dagon,* Hindus have *Matsya,* and we have *Kaala.* We're not the only ones to worship a god of the sea. We're not even the only ones in *Scot*land! Our brethren at Loch Ness have been worshipping Nessie for centuries.'

The rocks quaked beneath them. It was the first time John had felt it. *What was that?*

He looked around at the falling dust and steadied himself with his arms out and his legs apart. It reminded John of riding the underground when he'd visited London. The ground lurched and shook the same way the trains did. The room rattled around them. Rocks started to fall from within the cave. They hit the floor and shattered into shards.

Ben looked up at the falling rocks. 'This is the end... She's starting anew,' he said to himself. He then turned to look at John and said, 'Join us. These gods are real and there's nothing more we can do to appease them.'

'There's nothing you ever could have done to appease them. You had your own brother killed, and what good did it do? The so-called god you sacrificed him to is dead,' John said. 'Your only brother was killed, and it was all in vain.'

'Patrick was never my family. But these people...' he gestured to the hanging bodies of the dead worshippers around him, '...they were. We lived together, we worshipped together, and now, at the end of it all, we die together. I did what I had to do to help the people I love.' The ground shook again. Cracks stretched across the walls of the cave and more rocks fell. It rumbled like thunder as though they were in the heart of a storm. 'But what did you do? You left your family behind. You say that I'm a bad brother, but do you really think you're any better?'

John was speechless. Over the past thirty years he had created an image in his mind of his family being just as hateful and bigoted as the men who killed Patrick, but after spending this time with Sarah and seeing Victor's heartbreak over his son's death, he suddenly wondered if he should have given his family more credit. He hadn't been able to see it until now, but they loved him, and he loved them. He just needed to be able to hate them, and the island, in order to survive the pain of leaving them all behind. He wished things had been different. He wished he could have stayed and come out to his parents when he had the chance. Even if they struggled with it at first, he now felt that they eventually would have been happy for him. After all, Sarah had accepted him from the beginning. She was the one that discovered...

...John and Patrick had just gotten back from one of their long walks and were sitting in John's bedroom, eating crisps on his bed. They were laughing about something that Patrick had said - what it was, John couldn't remember - when Patrick had put his hand on John's and leaned towards him. John's heart leapt in his chest and he was certain that Patrick was about to kiss him. He'd never kissed anyone before but had thought about this moment often and had always hoped that Patrick had thought about it too. But just as Patrick leaned in, John's bedroom door burst open. Sarah, who was fourteen at the time, stood in the doorway, and when she realised what was happening, her jaw dropped.

John felt a wave of humiliation and fear crash over him and yanked his hand away from Patrick's.

'Please don't tell anyone,' John said to Sarah. His heart thumped harder than it ever had before.

But Sarah just stood there and looked at them both for what felt like an eternity. 'Do you love each other?' she finally asked.

John and Patrick shared a quick glance with each other and John could feel his face flush. He hadn't considered love. He hadn't let himself think about it in case Patrick didn't feel as strongly for him as he did for Patrick. All he knew was that when he was with him everything felt right and he was happy. But now he knew exactly how Patrick felt. They looked away from each other awkwardly and then looked back at Sarah. John couldn't help himself: he smiled.

Sarah squealed with childish glee and ran over to them. She jumped on the bed and gave them a massive, warm, loving hug. The kind that only a sister could give. It was then that John knew that Sarah...

...had accepted him. Sarah had always accepted and loved him, and instead of loving her back, he had turned his back on her. He had to do right by her. He needed to be a better brother. He'd get Sarah. They'd get on Victor's boat. They'd get off this island. They'd go to St. Andrews together. They'd start a new life as a family. They'd be happy.

'I hope to see you on the other side,' Ben said earnestly. 'I really hope you can forgive me, John. I really do.' He then looked up at the roof of the cave as though he was staring up into space and towards distant worlds. He then said something quietly to himself that John could just about hear over the distant rumbling. '"I came like Water, and like Wind I go."'

The ground quaked harder this time. The whole cave shook and nearly knocked John off his feet. With a sound like a roaring jet engine, the ground split and a large crack appeared in the middle of the chamber, right beneath Ben. The sound was deafening and was amplified by its echoes in the cave. Ben didn't have time to kick away the stepladder before the crack in the ground swallowed it from beneath his feet. He fell. It was supposed to be a clean drop and an instant death, but the quake caused the rope to swing instead. Ben dangled over the crevice and struggled with the noose around his neck.

'Ben!' John yelled.

Ben looked at John with bulging eyes and clawed at the rope as his head turned purple. His veins pulsed on the side of his neck.

The crack beneath him opened wider and rocks ricocheted off the sides as they fell into it. The dead worshipers fell to the ground as the wooden beams splintered and then snapped. Ben fell with them, but before he could die, he plummeted into the gaping hole beneath him. If the noose hadn't been so tight, he would have screamed.

John turned and ran as water started to rise up out of the crack, raising the bodies of the dead worshippers with it. Rocks dropped like bombs around him as he charged down the tunnel. The water was coming faster now, and he heard it rushing up behind him. Ben's corpse would soon follow.

He clambered up the stairs, on all fours like he had as a teenager, and ran into the temple. The altar crumbled with the quake. One of the walls collapsed. It hit the ground and its giant grey stones bounced over the cliff's edge and splashed into the ocean. John quickly leapt over a large stone that tumbled his way. The remains of the stained-glass window shattered.

When John got outside, he realised that it was raining. Clouds blackened the sky and a giant storm raged across the island. It was raining so hard that for a second, John feared another rain of fish.

John jumped into Sarah's car and put it in gear. The driver's seat was wet from where he had left the door open. As he pressed his foot on the accelerator the wheels spun in the mud beneath him.

Come on!

The wheels finally caught and John went flying away from the temple. He heard the ground quake even harder around him, and as he looked in the rear-view mirror, he saw the land beneath the temple crumble away and disappear into the sea below.

NINETEEN

The land shall join the sea.
From an ancient Hebridean prophecy.

John raced along the narrow island roads. The sky had darkened with thick angry clouds that swirled overhead. It was raining heavily. The wind grew stronger and the tall dead grass was almost horizontal as it bent in the wind. The island's trees, now completely dead, had been stripped of their leaves. They stood as naked as winter.

John looked through the passenger window and saw huge waves crashing into the cliffs on the coast. They raced like horses and exploded into white salty clouds as they broke against the rocks. The water rushed down the sides of the road, forming tiny rapids, carrying debris and the remains of the birds and fish in its wake. A thin, constant spray of water blew through the cracked windscreen and across John's face. It felt like running through fog.

This is it, John thought. *The island is finally dying. It's collapsing in on itself. Everything had been leading up to this moment. The fish, the birds… the god.*

A car suddenly appeared in front of him, speeding down the wrong side of the road. John jerked the wheel and swerved out of the way. The other car skidded on the wet road and disappeared out of sight. A moment later John heard it crash into a tree. There was no time to stop.

He slammed his foot on the brake outside of Sarah's shop. The car skidded uncontrollably. John jerked forward as the car finally stopped. He unbuckled his seatbelt and ran out of the car.

The door to the shop was locked. He peered inside. It was dark and empty.

'Sarah!' John yelled as he banged on the glass. No answer. She must have gone home.

John jumped back into the car and drove to Sarah's house. The street was full of people throwing whatever belongings they could grab into their cars. They were evacuating their homes. They knew what was happening. Even if they didn't fully understand the connection to the creature on the beach, they knew enough to know that they couldn't stay on the island. The ground quaked again as another part of the island was torn away.

One family of four jumped into their car with their border terrier and just left, leaving unloaded cases of luggage by a dry spot where their car had been parked. Even the dog looked worried as it peered out of the window as they drove away from their home.

John parked the car and ran inside his old family home.

'Sarah!' he shouted.

He was worried that she had already left but found her in the kitchen. She was standing by the window, staring at the apocalyptic scene outside.

'What's happening?' she asked. She was as terrified as everyone else.

John knew they didn't have much time, but he gave her a massive hug. He wrapped his arms tight around her, feeling her heart beat through her cardigan.

'I'm so sorry,' John said. 'I never should have left you the way I did. It was wrong. I should have told you where I was going.'

Sarah pulled back from the hug and looked into his eyes. Her own eyes filled with tears.

'You've loved me better than I've ever loved you,' John continued. Water dripped from his hair, across his face, 'and even after deserting you for thirty years you've shown me love that I simply don't deserve. You've welcomed me into your home and made me your brother again.' His kissed her on her forehead. 'Can you ever forgive me?'

Sarah squeezed him even tighter. She buried her face into his shoulder. This was all she had ever wanted, ever since John had left.

'Yes,' she said. She finally had her brother back. At long last, after years of grief and loneliness, she had a family again.

The ground trembled and then violently shook beneath them. Glasses fell from shelves and photo frames fell from the walls, crashing to the floor. The floor lurched, causing drawers and cabinets to burst open.

Sarah screamed as plates, pots, and pans crashed out of the cupboards.

'We have to go,' John said, grabbing her wrist.

'What's happening?' Sarah asked, following him as he pulled her.

'The island's falling apart,' John told her. 'Victor said that he had room on his boat.' He looked at his watch. It was almost noon. 'But we have to leave now. He's our only way off the island.'

'But he tried to kill us,' Sarah said.

'No,' John said. 'He was trying to *warn* us.'

John drove Sarah's car as fast as it would go. Its engine roared under the strain. The needle on the speedometer was struggling to reach eighty. The windows vibrated as they ran over the birds and fish that had been flattened into the roads.

The window wipers couldn't keep up with the downpour. Combined with the cracked glass, it was almost impossible to see. The rain was so heavy that it made the windscreen look like a dying television set, playing nothing but static.

A car shot past them and drove right through a puddle, spraying the car. Everyone was fleeing the island.

They drove down a residential street. Sarah pointed to a row of houses twenty metres away and shouted.

John saw the houses crumble and fall into the sea below. The ground forcefully shook beneath them and water exploded through cracks in the street, like geysers, bursting from the earth.

John swerved the car to avoid the widening cracks in the road. He drove up onto a grassy bank and skidded down the other side to avoid the water erupting from the ground.

As they got closer to the harbour the road became jammed with traffic. The cars stood still, top to tail. Horns blasted. Lights flashed. People screamed at each other over the thunderous sound of cracking earth. It was total mayhem.

John saw a man pull his family out of their car, forcing them to leave their luggage behind. He saw another man, staring comatose out to sea as his screaming wife was tugging on his arm, unable to get him to move. She eventually ran away, leaving him staring into oblivion.

'Come on,' John said. 'We've got to run.'

They jumped out of the car and left the engine running. Others followed suit, abandoning their vehicles and their belongings, as they raced towards the harbour.

The waves were ferocious. The boats bounced up and down over the waves as they rolled beneath them and crashed into the harbour. Some boats had already made it out to sea but they weren't faring any better. The water was just as rough. Out at sea, John saw a boat disappear and hoped that it had just been obscured by a large wave, but in his gut, he knew that it hadn't.

'Do you know which boat is Victor's?' Sarah shouted over the noise. John didn't. They ran through the harbour. Waves crashed against the wood of the dock as they ran, almost knocking them off their feet.

John glanced at his watch. It was about to strike noon, but the sky was as dark as night. If he were Victor, he would have already left.

'Victor!' John shouted desperately over the wall of noise that surrounded them. 'Victor, where are you?'

John thought he heard someone respond, but the waves and the wind were so loud he couldn't be sure. He looked around him.

'John?'

It was Victor's voice. Where was he?

John looked through the driving rain, and just a few metres away he saw Victor standing on a small fishing boat tied to the wooden dock, waving his arms at them. The tiny boat rode up and down on the waves. John didn't have high hopes of the boat leaving the harbour, let alone making it all the way to the mainland, but it was their only chance of escape. John and Sarah ran to him.

'Get on!' Victor shouted. He supported himself by the side of his boat and held out his hand for John to take.

The boat jerked up and down as it was shaken by the waves. It rose and fell a metre at a time. John waited for the boat to level with the dock. He grabbed Victor's hand and jumped on. Victor yanked him over the side. John hit the deck of the boat. Pain ripped through his shoulder and down his arm as he landed in an inch of water.

'I can't do it,' Sarah said. The boat was rocking too fast for her to jump on. John held on to the side of the boat and got to his feet.

She bent her knees, ready to jump, but no sooner had the boat levelled it had jerked away again.

'Yes, you can!' John shouted. 'As soon as it's level, just jump.'

The boat dropped beneath the pier and then rose up. Sarah went to jump and backed out at the last second. 'I can't!' she cried.

'Jump on as the boat drops past you,' Victor said.

'We've got you,' John said.

She waited. The boat jerked up with the wave and as the wave passed beneath the boat it dropped below the dock.

Sarah leapt. She jumped onto the boat and John caught her in his arms. They both fell to the deck. John thumped his head against the floor. Sarah lay on top of him as she tried to catch her breath.

'I told you, you could do it,' John said, wincing through the pain. His head throbbed from where it hit the deck.

'Alright, let's go!' Victor said and cut the rope that was holding them to the dock. There was no time to untie it. 'Everyone in the cabin.'

The cabin was tiny. There were two seats, one in front of the wheel and one beside it. Victor sat behind the steering wheel and John let Sarah sit beside Victor. John shut the door and stood with his back to the wall, holding on to the back of Sarah's chair to keep himself from falling. He stood with his legs apart, trying to steady himself as best as he could.

Victor started the engine. The boat roared to life and he manoeuvred them as quickly, and as safely, as he could out of the harbour.

'I was worried you wouldn't make it,' Victor said.

'So was I,' John told him.

Wallace Burns was woken up by an almighty crack of thunder. He jerked up from the hard plastic bed that he had been sleeping on. His body was covered in scratches. Many of them were still bleeding.

'The plane's crashing!' Wallace shouted as he leapt out of bed. The shaking of his cell felt like severe turbulence. Before he could wake up and realise what was happening, he was jerked up and down. His stomach lurched, and he sprayed vomit all over the wall. It quickly dawned on him that he wasn't on an aeroplane at all. He was still in his cell.

He ran to the door and shouted through the flap. 'What's going on?' He banged on the cell door to get someone's attention. 'Mitchell! Help!' But the police station was empty. Mitchell's body had disappeared into the sea with the temple as it crumbled away, and the rest of the staff at the station had fled at the first sign of danger. No one had bothered to let Wallace out, or even to wake him up. He was trapped, stuck in his concrete tomb.

The ground shook again and the walls cracked.

Wallace jumped. He pressed his back to the door. The whole room tilted and heaved. He fell to his knees and felt his kneecap crack as it struck the concrete floor.

Ice cold water began to spray through the crack into the cell. Wallace jumped out of the way of the stream, but then realised that he might be able to escape. He ran to where the water was coming in and clawed at the crack in the wall, trying to pry it apart with his fingers. Maybe he could break out. Maybe he would be okay. He forced his hands into the crack, got a handhold on the jagged stone, and pulled as hard as he could, feeling the muscles in his arms tear at the force, but the water kept spraying in and his fingers slipped. He caught fingernails on both hands against the rough edge of the crack and they snapped backwards, ripping away from his fingers.

'Argh!'

The ground quaked again and another crack formed beneath him. Water flooded into his cell. The water looked as though it was rapidly boiling as it bubbled up, filling the cell. The icy water was making his feet numb.

'Help!' Wallace screamed with such force that he thought that he had made his throat bleed. The water was rising fast and he didn't care about anything other than escaping. In moments, the water was up to his neck, and seconds later it had lifted him off his feet toward the ceiling. It was so cold it felt like his breath was being torn from his lungs. Wallace swam over to the crack for a desperate last attempt to free himself, but as he tried to kick, he couldn't feel his legs. The water was just too cold. A moment later he couldn't feel his arms either.

'Help me!' he screamed, without anyone hearing. 'Help me!' The water finally covered his mouth.

Wallace tried to hold his breath, but he had used the last of his oxygen screaming for help. His body forced him to take a deep breath in and salty water filled his lungs. As his heart beat for the final time, Wallace only thought of two things: Claire, and his whisky.

TWENTY

She will awaken.
From an ancient Hebridean prophecy.

Victor steered his fishing boat away from the island. The boat bounced over the waves. The skeleton of St. Budoc's Island stood behind them like a prehistoric totem disintegrating into the sea. The hills crumbled like sandcastles and the cliffs crashed into the sea.

A moment after Victor steered his boat away from the wooden pier, it broke apart and collapsed into the water, pulling the people on it into the icy water of the harbour. The people tried to scramble up the sides of the boats that remained, but the waves overpowered them and dragged them under. Others looked in horror as they stood in the car park of the harbour, realising that their only hope of escape had just crumbled before their eyes.

The water was heaving, and the waves were high, so Victor couldn't go as fast as he wanted to. He gripped the wheel and carefully navigated the boat over the swells, but the boat lurched forward and jerked to the side as a wave caught them off guard. Sarah almost slipped from her seat, but John caught her with one hand, gripping the back of her chair with the other until his knuckles turned blue.

A motorboat a hundred metres in front of them struck a wave head on and flipped over on itself. It crashed onto the surface of the water and quickly submerged. The boat resurfaced a second later with no evidence of its passengers.

As he passed by, Victor kept his eye out for anyone in the water. John looked out of the window as they sped away, trying to see if anyone would bob back up to the surface, but there was no one there. After only a few seconds he lost sight of the boat. The waters had become too rough. The sea was fighting against them.

When they crested the next wave, the three of them saw that they were surrounded by about twenty to thirty other boats, all trying to flee. Out of all the boats that had been moored at the harbour, less than half of them had been able to escape.

How many people are still on the island? John thought.

Some of the boats they saw were small, like Victor's fishing boat, but others were much larger and could hold ten or fifteen people. They had even passed a woman in a kayak, who was frantically paddling and traversing the waves quite successfully, or so John thought.

'Can we help her?' John asked, pointing to the woman.

'Who?' Victor asked and looked to where John was pointing. The water was now empty. She was nowhere to be seen.

'Where did she go?' John said. His eyes darted over the waves where she and her kayak once were. There was nothing left but the dark waves.

Something struck a fishing boat to their left, causing the boat to lurch out of the water and crash back down on its side, breaking in half. They were too far away from them, and the water was too rough, to hear their screams. John thought he saw at least three people fly into the air before crashing into the waves and disappearing.

'What hit them?' Sarah shrieked. She was hyperventilating. 'What was that?'

'It's okay,' Victor said. 'We're all going to be fine.'

As he spoke, lightning struck the water in front of them and for a split second it was as bright as a summer's day. The water turned a vibrant aqua where the lightning had struck, making it look like pool water, and the flash illuminated the large white yacht in front of them. Something long and thin had emerged from the water, raised thirty feet into the air, and had come crashing down onto the boat, tearing it apart.

John thought that it looked like a tentacle and thought back to the tableau carved into the wall of the tunnel beneath the temple.

Dear God, I hope I'm wrong, John prayed.

The sea returned to darkness, leaving the shape of the lightning burned onto John's retina and the yacht burst into flames before it sank beneath the waves. Black smoke rose from the flaming rubble and leaking oil caught alight as it spread over the water.

'She's here...' Victor murmured. His eyes widened as he scanned the water. He turned the wheel to avoid the flaming debris and whatever it was that had reached out from beneath the waves.

'Who's here?' Sarah asked nervously.

Neither Victor nor John answered her. They didn't dare.

One by one the boats around them disappeared, and John's panic reached a new height. 'Can this thing go any faster?' he asked. He felt the boat vibrate. It wasn't just the rain or waves that was making it shake. The engine was struggling. It made a loud mechanical whine as it fought against the waves.

Sarah looked from where the yacht had been and turned to John. Her eyes were illuminated with fear and he could tell she was thinking the same thing that he was: they weren't going to last much longer. She reached out to him. John grabbed her hand and held it tight. For a second, everything felt all right. Brother and sister together again.

Victor said, 'She's going as fast as she—'

A huge black tentacle slammed down into the middle of the boat. Unlike the boat beside them, theirs wasn't big enough to snap in half, and instead, it was dragged into the darkness beneath the waves. Bubbles erupted from the cabin as water replaced the air inside.

As they went under, Victor was thrown forward and smashed his face against the metal window frame. The blunt force of the collision killed him instantly. He didn't even have time to realise what was happening.

In just a few seconds, the freezing water flooded the cabin, and before they could understand what was happening, both Sarah and John were underwater.

Victor's corpse floated up from its seat and Sarah screamed. A fury of bubbles escaped her lungs. As soon as she tasted the salty water, she shut her mouth. She looked for John through the water but as the icy water stung her eyes she found it difficult to see anything.

John had experience swimming in such cold water, but normally he'd be wearing a wetsuit, which would only take a little while to warm up. As it filled the cabin, the water turned colder and colder by the second, and the light from above the water continued to fade as the boat sank. Except for a small red light on the control panel, the cabin was completely black.

It's pulling us down, John thought. *Whatever It is.*

John found Sarah's hand in the dark and held onto it as tightly as he could. He refused to let her go.

We can make it, John thought. If he couldn't speak to reassure her then he would at least try to convince himself.

He felt around for the door, but when he found it the water pressure was so strong that it wouldn't open. It was as though it had been bolted shut. The only other option was to smash the glass. It was dangerous, but John had to do something. His ears had popped twice since being dragged underwater and he could tell that they were descending fast.

John let go of Sarah's hand – he'd take it again once he busted the glass windows open - and held on to the back of Victor's seat. He lifted his legs in the water and kicked against the glass with both feet. He kicked it over and over again, but his legs dragged in the water and it felt like they were moving in slow-motion. After one tremendous kick, the glass shattered and the whole pane broke outwards.

John grabbed hold of Sarah's hand again. She thrashed in the water. She was panicking.

Calm down! John willed his thoughts into Sarah's mind. He could just about see her. Her dark hair floated around her face like spider legs in the dim red light and her free hand was clawing at the ceiling of the cabin.

John tried to pull her through the smashed glass behind him. Sharp edges caught his shoulders and he felt warm blood escape his body. He pulled at Sarah's hand to guide her through the window. Her hand held his tightly but she didn't move.

Sarah looked up at him in panic and motioned towards her legs. Her feet were caught on something beneath the chair, but John couldn't see what it was.

With his legs floating out of the smashed window behind him, John held on to both of Sarah's hands and pulled as hard as he could, but he couldn't get her to budge.

John's heart leapt with fear and he started to swim back through the window to free Sarah's leg, but he felt her grip loosen. She couldn't hold on to him anymore. He found her face and grabbed it with both hands, looking into her eyes and willing her to hold on. He could just make out the whites of her eyes in the darkness, but her eyes didn't look back at him.

Come on! John thought.

Sarah went limp and her face slipped from John's hands. She pulled away from him as the boat sank. John could just barely see the red glow of the cabin light as Sarah sank below him. The last John saw of his beautiful sister were her eyes and open mouth staring up at him in the depths of the sea, begging for him to help her. Just before the boat disappeared, John saw a giant tentacle wrapped around it, dragging it down.

John tried to call after her, but she was too far down. He kicked his legs as hard as he could, trying to follow the boat into the darkness. He could still save her. He knew he could. He had to. He kicked hard, but it was difficult to tell if he was making any progress. If only he had his flippers on. If only he had his SCUBA gear. He felt like he was trapped in a nightmare, forever swimming but never moving.

The cold and darkness around him started to make John feel confused and faint. He suddenly felt thirsty. No, not thirsty. Hungry. No, not hungry... he needed to breathe. He was suffocating. He couldn't remember how long he had been holding his breath, but suddenly he knew he couldn't hold on for much longer. His muscles ached and his entire body seized up. His chest felt like it was bursting, and the sensation travelled from his lungs up through his throat and into his head, where his temples violently throbbed. He was desperate. He needed air. His lungs begged him to take a breath.

Sarah...

He looked down into the darkness where she had fallen and then looked up at the surface. There was a faint fiery light. Debris burned above him in the distance. The surface was too far away.

How deep am I? he thought. *20 metres? 40? More?*

He was running out of oxygen and would never make it that far. There was another flash of lightning above him and the thunder that followed shook the water, sounding like a bomb had gone off in the distance. In the brief flash of light, John saw the bodies of the dead around him, sinking into the infinite terror of the darkness below. Ships sank below them. They looked like they were moving in slow motion, but maybe John was sinking with them.

His ears popped again. The water pressure was too much. He felt a sharp sting race through his head, from ear to ear. He couldn't cope with the pressure. He'd never been this deep before.

John kicked as hard as he could, facing what he hoped was the surface. His thoughts felt far away and it was getting hard to know where he was anymore. He made no progress. Despite all his kicking, he was still sinking, and he was sinking fast.

The water became colder and colder around him. He started to lose feeling in his toes and fingers. It felt like stepping inside a walk-in freezer.

He needed to breathe. The pain was too much for him. His lungs were desperate to get rid of the carbon dioxide in his body, but John knew that if he exhaled he wouldn't be able to keep himself from inhaling again, and that would be the end. There was another flash of lightning and John involuntarily let out a small amount of air. His bubbles came out of his mouth like strange gaseous jellyfish and shot towards the surface like a bullet.

And then something appeared before him. What was left of the light from the surface was obscured, and the darkness beneath him rose to meet him, like a tangible shadow. The thing hovered only metres before him and filled John's entire field of vision.

The face of the new god emerged before his eyes.

It was a colossal, cephalopodic abomination– a huge creature with equally huge tentacles that rose up around its body like unhallowed seaweed. Some of its tentacles reached the surface, and some floated beneath him. They seemed to fill the entire ocean. The creature was in front of John but was so huge that it also seemed to surround him.

Its face drew closer to John. John could just about make it out as his eyes struggled to see in the dark. Its giant eye shimmered with unseen light. It had a huge horizontal slit for a pupil, which was twice, or three times, as wide as John was tall. Its eye was not quite like that of an octopus, nor of a squid. It was unlike any eye John had ever encountered in all of his research, and more torturous than any nightmare would ever dare include. There was only one word that came close to describing the thing before him: *blasphemous.*

It was the antithesis of human.

John floated before it, unable to move. He was suspended in place and could only stare at the horror before him as the cold bore into his unblinking eyes. The depths of the sea gripped him with its icy tendrils, forcing him to see.

He stared into the eye of the new god. Its pupil dilated and then contracted, as though it was intrigued by John. It was watching him – *studying* him – and John could feel that it wasn't only seeing him but seeing *into* him.

John's cheeks bulged with his final breath. This was the scientific discovery of a lifetime, but he wished he had never seen it. He wished he could be elsewhere, back at his university teaching, back in his bed at his home in St. Andrews, even back at his family home with Sarah.

Sarah…

His dream of starting a new life with his sister now lay in the depths of the sea. He had been teased by it and had even dared to be excited by it, but now it was nothing but a foolish dream. He was foolish to have hoped for a happy life. First Patrick had been taken from him, then Lawrence had died before his eyes, and now Sarah was gone, after he had just gotten her back.

He'd no longer be able to show her his home, his university, or the life he had built for himself on the mainland. He pictured himself back home, helping Sarah look for a new house, a new car, a new job… but it was all gone. He couldn't help Sarah with anything anymore.

The thing that hurt him more than any of that, though, was the realisation that he would no longer be able to be a brother. He hadn't realised how desperately he needed family until he had returned to St. Budoc's. He had spent the last few decades believing that he was doing fine on his own. He'd been single his whole adult life and hadn't allowed himself to fall in love again. He had good working relationships with his colleagues and his students, but he had always been careful not to get too close to any of them, and didn't have any real friends or family on the mainland. He didn't realise just how alone he had been.

Now he felt that his last chance of having a family had been snatched away from him. His sister was somewhere in the darkness below, dragged away by whatever unholy god hovered before him.

The pressure on John's face was too strong. His final breath escaped him. The bubbles scrambled away from his mouth and disappeared into the water above him. Instinctively, he tried to breathe. His body wouldn't wait any longer. He took a deep, desperate breath, and frigid water poured into his lungs.

The cold tore through him from the inside out. He tried to fight it by exhaling again, trying to push the water out of his lungs, but it was no use. It felt like he was choking on ice.

John writhed in the water until a warming sensation slowly filled his body from his feet all the way to the top of his head. He felt dizzy at first, but then he felt peaceful. His body stopped convulsing and his eyes drifted in and out of focus as he stared into the black of the monster's eye.

The god was still watching John as he floated in a strange limbo. John hovered in the water, still conscious but slowly slipping away. It was both agonising and tranquil at the same time. Half of him wanted to relax and let go, and the other half of him wanted to fight and swim, but he felt like he had no energy to do either.

The god raised a tentacle from the hidden depths of the darkness below and John watched passively as it snaked towards him and found his mouth. It was thick and black, as though it was made from darkness itself, and glistened in what little light could reach this far down.

It touched John's lips.

It was slick and smooth, and felt more like oil than something solid. John remembered the membrane that covered the creature on the beach. This was worse. The tentacle pushed against John's mouth and in dazed horror John concentrated what was left of his energy in holding his mouth shut.

No! Leave me alone!

As though it could hear his thoughts, the tentacle pulled back. It floated inches away from his face, moving like a curious snake. But John's energy was fading, and just as his mouth fell slack the tentacle jolted forward, past his lips, into his mouth, and down into the back of his throat.

John's whole body seized up and he tried to gag, but the thing slithered down his throat and reached into his water-logged lungs. His mouth and nose were filled with the taste of petrol and rotting fish and he felt like he was both drowning and choking. He tried to lift his hands to pull the tentacle out of his mouth, but his arms wouldn't move. He could no longer feel them. He wanted to vomit, to escape, to do anything, but John had lost all control over his body and his consciousness was slipping away. The only thing he was aware of now was the feeling of the thick, slug-like tentacle forcing its way down his throat, stretching his windpipe. His throat and chest felt like they were tearing open and his body was screaming for air. John tried to turn off his mind, to disconnect himself from his body and let himself slip into unconsciousness. He wanted to die. He wanted this nightmare to be over but all he could do was watch.

John looked in horror at the god before him.

The god looked back.

TWENTY-ONE

The joy of a loved one is like spring for the soul.
An old Hebridean proverb.

'It's rude to point,' the boy said.

John looked down at his underwear, which stretched out at the front. Embarrassment flooded through him. He grabbed his bag and held it in front of himself to hide his shame. The boy lunged toward him and yanked it away, throwing it across the changing room and almost hitting another kid in the face.

'No need to hide it,' he said. 'Let the world see what you really are!'

The boys in the changing room all laughed at him. Someone threw a shoe and it smacked John on the side of his head. He turned to see who had thrown it, but it could have been anyone.

Patrick watched sympathetically but was powerless to help.

John tried to ignore the boys' jeers and scrambled to get his uniform back on. He had just about managed to pull his trousers back on but gave up on the rest. He grabbed his shirt and his shoes and ran out of the changing room. He felt like he could still hear their laughter as he disappeared out of the school grounds and fled down the road.

John lay down on his bed. His feet almost reached the bottom of it now. In a few more years he'd need to get a bigger one. He stared up at the textured ceiling and listened to the sounds of his family downstairs. He couldn't see any shapes in the ceiling, not today.

There was a knock at the front door. A few seconds later Fran Calvary, John's mother, opened the front door and called up to him. 'John!'

'Yeah?' John called back. He didn't want to see anyone or speak to anyone. He just wanted to hide in his room. He was planning on being sick tomorrow and staying at home. He was sure he could fake a high temperature if he needed to.

'It's for you!' Fran yelled back.

John deflated. He just wanted to curl up and disappear beneath his blankets. He hauled himself out of bed. His body felt heavy and he had a killer headache. He stood up and plodded down the stairs. Fran was talking to whoever was at the front door. She was wearing a chunky knitted cardigan.

She looked up at John, smiled, and said, 'I'll leave you two to it.' She disappeared back into the house and started making noise in the kitchen, most likely preparing dinner.

Standing in the doorway, smiling at him, was Patrick. He was sixteen and still in his school uniform of grey trousers and a white shirt.

'Hi John,' Patrick said.

'Hi...' John said, confused.

Patrick and John walked across old Isherwood's farm. As they walked through the field the sheep edged away with caution. They watched them from a safe distance and moved whenever they deemed that the two boys were getting too close. The sheep bleated disapprovingly.

It was a beautiful day. The sky was blue with giant fluffy clouds hovering in the distance. Sunlight poured over the grass and there was only a faint breeze blowing over the island. There were only two or three truly sunny days in the year on St. Budoc's Island, and that day was one of them. They walked for a few minutes, soaking up the sun and chatting about school, music, and local gossip, and then they walked for a few more minutes in silence, simply enjoying each other's presence.

'Can I ask you something?' Patrick asked after a while. 'Something personal?'

John swallowed. 'It depends on what it is,' he said with a nervous chuckle.

Patrick slowed down but kept walking. He glanced over to John beside him and then asked, 'Are you...' he paused, and looked away as he tried to find the right words to say. 'Do you like boys?'

John stiffened. He immediately became defensive and said, 'No.' He scrunched up his face as proof that he was disgusted at the thought.

'Oh,' Patrick said, shying away in embarrassment. 'Okay. I'm sorry. Never mind.' They continued to walk in silence.

'What made you think that?' John asked a while later.

'Earlier at school...' Patrick started.

John looked at him blankly.

'When we were in the changing rooms—'

'I'm not gay,' John said. Embarrassment flushed his cheeks and turned them into two rosy circles.

Patrick held up his hands. 'Okay, okay, I believe you,' he said. 'It's just that, if you were…' he thought for a moment and then added, '…that would be okay.'

John looked at him. Was he trying to tell him something? Was Patrick someone he could trust? Maybe… He wasn't sure. Could he open up to him? He thought so. He *hoped* so.

'Are you?' John asked.

Patrick looked at the flock of sheep in front of them as they edged away, clearing a path for Patrick and John to walk through. Then he turned to look back at John. He studied his face intently. Patrick then smiled and quietly said, 'I might be…'

They kept walking for another half an hour before heading home. Patrick's house was closer, so they went there first. As they stood by the front door, Patrick said, 'Thank you.'

'What for?' John asked.

'For not judging me,' Patrick said and smiled.

From an upstairs window, Ben Walters pulled back the curtain and secretly watched them from above. He saw Patrick give John a hug. It was a deeper hug than a friend might normally give, and it lasted a moment too long. Patrick kissed John on the cheek.

John pulled away from him. 'What are you doing?' he said, flustered. He looked around to make sure that no one had seen Patrick kiss him. If he had looked upwards he would have seen Ben staring down at them in shock.

Ben dropped the curtain shut. Neither John nor Patrick noticed that Ben had been watching.

Most days after school, John and Patrick would go for a long walk. They'd take a different route each day but would always head for a field or farmland hidden away where no one could see them. That late in the day, most of the farmers had finished up, so their fields were the most secluded places on the island. It was almost guaranteed that John and Patrick would be safe and alone there.

It took John a few weeks, but he eventually found the courage to reach out and hold Patrick's hand. It was gentle at first. The backs of their hands would brush as they walked. And then they lingered.

Eventually, their fingers found each other, like long lost friends. It was scary for them both but holding Patrick's hand made John happier than he thought he could be.

Electricity surged through John's body as he looked away, too scared to look at either Patrick or their embraced hands. He smiled to himself a happy, giddy little smile.

John sat in Mr. Sutherland's classroom as he spoke, slowly, explaining the process of photosynthesis. John was drawing in his notebook. He had been taking notes but became distracted and had turned his attention to a drawing of a diver in an old-style diving suit, standing at the bottom of the ocean. His oxygen line stretched from his helmet to the surface as simply-drawn fish swam around him.

One day, John thought. *One day, I'll learn to dive underwater.*

The night before, he had watched *The Undersea World of Jacques Cousteau,* an old French documentary series that the BBC were airing. He went to sleep dreaming of fish and woke up as though all of the world's problems had melted away.

He looked up from his notebook and glanced at Patrick. Patrick smiled at him. John felt butterflies flutter within him. He smiled back. Everything was right with the world.

The bell rang, marking the end of the day, and the pupils packed their books into their bags and began to file out of the classroom, ready to head home.

'John, Patrick,' Mr. Sutherland said. 'Can you stay behind for a minute?'

John and Patrick shared a worried glance with each other. What could he want? They didn't speak at all during class, so they couldn't think of why they would be in trouble.

As the last pupil left the classroom Mr. Sutherland asked her to close the door and she shut it behind her. It was just the three of them now.

He waited a moment, looking from John to Patrick and back to John again. Then he spoke in his deep, slow voice.

'I would like to talk to you about something quite personal,' Mr. Sutherland said, 'but I'd rather not do it here, where others might overhear. Do you have to rush off home this afternoon?'

'No, Sir,' they both said, almost in unison.

'Excellent,' Mr. Sutherland said. He looked at them both with a warm smile, as if to reassure them that everything was fine. 'Give me a minute to gather my things and I'll meet you in my office.'

Patrick and John waited for Mr. Sutherland outside of his office. They sat on uncomfortable wooden chairs that were lined up against the wall. Most of the pupils had gone home and only a few teachers stayed this long after school had finished. The walls were decorated with artwork that pupils had painted in art class, along with some educational posters that the school had bought too long ago for them to still be scientifically correct. John was nervous. Despite Mr. Sutherland's friendly behaviour, his smile had been too tight to be genuine.

'Do you know what this is about?' Patrick whispered.

John shrugged, chewing on the inside of his lip. He had no idea. They both just sat still, with their legs crossed, staring at the posters on the wall in front of them.

Mr. Sutherland lumbered down the hallway. Carrying that much weight around his stomach looked exhausting, but somehow he managed. He nodded at the boys, unlocked the door to his office, and welcomed them in.

'Thanks for waiting behind,' he said. 'Please, take a seat.' He gestured to the two chairs in front of his desk. These ones had fabric cushioning on the seats.

Mr. Sutherland shut the door behind them and let out a huge chesty cough.

John heard a click.

Did he just lock the door?

Mr. Sutherland lumbered over to the corner of his office and put a kettle on to boil. He waited for it to boil and then poured the water into a teapot and dropped in several teabags. John and Patrick sat in silence whilst Mr. Sutherland casually, and without urgency, finished brewing the pot of tea. He brought it over to his desk on a tray, with two petite china cups.

The air in the office felt thick. It smelled of dust and old books. Rooms always felt heavier when the headmaster was present. He had a gravitas that was indescribable, but distinctly palpable.

Mr. Sutherland placed the tray down on the desk and sat down, grabbing hold of the desk and huffing as he lowered himself into his chair. John noticed that the arms on his chair had been taken off to accommodate his size. Mr. Sutherland picked up the teapot and poured it into the two cups.

'Cup of tea?' Mr Sutherland asked with a smile.

'Yes please, Sir,' Patrick said.

'Not for me, thank you, Sir,' John said.

'Oh, don't be silly, I insist,' Mr. Sutherland said. He spoke smoothly and with conviction. 'Please, there's no reason to feel uncomfortable. I know it's scary being called into the *headmaster's* office but please, right now just think of me as your friend.'

His tone was meant to be comforting, but it had the opposite effect on John. He handed the two boys a cup of tea, one at a time. Each cup sat on a little saucer with a delicate pattern of waves around the rim.

'There you go, boys,' Mr. Sutherland said. 'Drink up.'

John took a sip of his tea. It was hot. He blew over it whilst stirring it to cool it down and took another sip. The warmth filled him up from the inside. It tasted herbal.

Patrick stirred two sugar cubes into his cup with a small silver teaspoon. The spoon clinked against the cup like a muted wind chime. He followed John's suit and blew over the top of his tea to cool it down.

'So,' Mr. Sutherland said after a few moments, 'it's been brought to my attention that you two have started a special kind of friendship.' He slowly looked from Patrick to John.

John froze. He quickly glanced over at Patrick, who averted his eyes.

How could he know? John thought. *We've been so careful…*

'Please,' Mr. Sutherland said. 'There's no need to worry!'

That made John tense up even more.

'If there's no need to worry, why have you called us into your office?' Patrick asked.

'So, you admit it?' Mr. Sutherland asked.

'I don't know what I'm admitting to…' Patrick said.

John didn't answer. He kept his eyes on his teacup as he took another sip. He didn't know what else to do, and he certainly didn't want to admit to anything. It had been hard enough to admit it to himself, and then it was even harder to admit it to Patrick.

'Oh, come on, boys, you can't form a relationship on uncertainty,' Mr. Sutherland said. 'The reason I wanted to talk to you two is to congratulate you.'

That shocked John even more. He looked over at Patrick, who looked just as uncertain. Mr. Sutherland was not the warmest of people and had been known to call up the parents of dating pupils if he saw any hint of their relationship at school. He had even held an assembly about how school was a place for studying and not for romance.

'Sir?' John said, looking up from his cup. He had drunk most of his tea already.

'It's difficult to understand who you truly are, especially if it's someone that you don't think society wants you to be,' Mr. Sutherland continued, 'but the fact that the pair of you have both happened upon this self-discovery, and can share it with each other, is absolutely wonderful.' He smiled when he said *'wonderful'*. It was a broad smile that revealed all his teeth, but never reached his eyes. It reminded John of the Cheshire Cat.

Something was off. John wasn't quite sure what it was, but he doubted that the headmaster called them to his office just to congratulate them on their 'special friendship.' He was uncomfortable and thought that it was probably time to leave.

Patrick finished his tea with a final gulp.

As John finished his own cup of tea, and was planning on telling Mr. Sutherland that they had to go, the headmaster dropped out of focus for a second. Then he seemed to drift apart, forming two different people sitting in front of him. Mr. Sutherland's voice became deep and clean. It sounded like fresh water on a hot summer's day and then it began to drift far into the distance until it almost disappeared, like he was in a different room to them.

'Are you alright, Patrick?' Mr. Sutherland asked as his face swirled. His voice became increasingly muffled.

John looked over to Patrick. The whole room was moving around him. Patrick swayed in his chair, leaning from side to side. Patrick's eyes drooped shut and he passed out. Patrick hit his shoulder against Mr. Sutherland's desk as he slumped out of his chair and fell awkwardly to the floor.

Patrick! John tried to shout but he couldn't make a sound. He looked over at Mr. Sutherland. *What's happening?*

'You don't look too good yourself, boy…' Mr. Sutherland said. It was almost inaudible. Mr. Sutherland's desk felt incredibly long and his face continued to swirl in the distance.

John looked down at his cup.

It slipped out of his hand and smashed onto the floor. He looked back up at Mr. Sutherland for help, unable to speak. Mr. Sutherland stared back at him. His features floated around his face and he was no longer smiling. The world suddenly turned black as John slipped unconscious and fell to the floor.

The next thing John remembered was being shaken up and down. Footsteps trod beneath him. He was being carried. He tried to open his eyes but couldn't. They were glued shut. He tried again and managed to force them open ever so slightly. In his dazed stupor, the world was out of focus. There were vague shapes of people walking around him.

His vision drifted into focus. He saw Patrick being carried by a man beside him. He was limp in the man's arms.

Patrick! John wanted to shout for him but couldn't make a sound.

His body had failed him. He couldn't move, or even think straight. *Where are they taking us?*

He rolled his eyes to the front to look ahead of him and saw an ancient structure he'd never seen before. It looked like a church or a temple.

Everything went black.

When John opened his eyes, he was underneath the temple. It felt like he had merely blinked, but he must have been passed out for quite some time, as he was now being carried through a long dark tunnel. He could just about make out strange writing carved into the walls.

He blinked.

When he opened his eyes, he was lying in a shallow pool of cold seawater. The vague shapes of people stood above him, watching, but he couldn't make out their faces. Everything was out of focus. His head lolled to the side and he could see Patrick, screaming. His face was being held underwater. His nose, mouth and left eye were totally submerged. The water bubbled as he screamed for help but John couldn't do a thing. The large, blurred shape of a man kneeled on Patrick's back. His hand held Patrick's head in the water.

John's heart began to race, but his muscles still wouldn't move.

Patrick! he tried to scream again. His mouth opened ever so slightly but not far enough to make a sound.

John no longer cared about the others in the cave. The only person he could focus on was Patrick, being drowned in the water.

He heard a voice he didn't recognise. It echoed in the cave.

'We offer these boys unto you! Please accept them as our sacrifice.'

John looked helplessly at Patrick. Patrick, terrified, locked eyes with John and threw the man holding him down off his back and jerked his head out of the water in a panic.

'I saw it!' Patrick yelled. Water and spit coughed up from his mouth. 'I saw it! Dear God, I saw it! It's coming!' His eyes were wild with fear. 'What is that thing? My God, it's hideous! What did you make me see?'

Two other men joined the man who was struggling to hold Patrick down and they completely submerged his face in the water. Patrick screamed bubbles into the shallow pool.

John tried to move his body. He found enough energy to move his arm a fraction. Whatever Mr. Sutherland had put in his tea seemed to be wearing off.

John tried to shout but no words would come out. *No!* he wanted to scream. *Leave him alone! I love him! I love him! I love him!*

John looked around him. At the far end of the tunnel, he saw the stone stairs that led up to a wooden door. He only had one shot at this. If he tried to escape and failed, that would be it. He would be killed. Was he certain that he could do this? Was he absolutely sure that he could muster up enough strength to make a run for it? He had to try, and he had to do it now. He couldn't stay there whilst he watched Patrick die.

I'm sorry, Patrick, John thought as he pushed himself up and ran for the stairs.

TWENTY-TWO

God breathed life into the creatures of the sea,
But the creatures of the sea chose to walk on the earth.
From *Breith*, an early Hebridean creation story.

John's face contorted with agony and fear as the tentacle probed inside his chest. Everything he had just seen had looked so clear. It didn't feel like a memory, but like he had been back, reliving the past with Patrick. As the vision faded away, John felt like he had been jerked awake from a deep sleep. Reliving the past and watching Patrick die was terrifying. Waking up was worse.

He was awake, but the tentacle was still buried deep in his chest. The god had a hold of John and was watching him, studying him. Only it wasn't just looking with its eyes, it was looking with something much greater: something that could see deep inside the depths of John's heart and mind.

He remembered the eyes of the creature on West Beach – *Kaala's eyes* – and the all-knowing appearance they seemed to have.

The god's pupil contracted as it stared deeply into John, and John felt an overwhelming sense of sympathy wrap around him like a blanket, warming him from the inside out. The water no longer felt cold, but like a warm bath. John suddenly felt not just seen, but known.

Has the god taken pity on me?

As soon as the thought crossed his mind his lungs filled up with air. He felt the tentacle swell inside him as air flowed into his lungs and bubbled from his nose.

The god breathed life into John. Oxygen poured out of the tentacle and filled his lungs, displacing the water that he had inhaled moments before. He tried to cough, his chest heaving with each attempt, but the tentacle stayed in place, moving with John's body. His heart, which had slowed almost to a stop, started to pound within his chest, delivering the fresh oxygen to his starved cells. He could feel his hands and legs again. He could move his fingers. He could feel the water around him continue to warm up, and his fingers and toes began to tingle and burn as they warmed. John's instincts told him to yank the tentacle out of his mouth and swim up to the surface as fast as he could. But the moment he had that thought, something convinced him otherwise.

Stay...

John slowly began to rise as the god lifted him to the surface with its tentacle still inside his mouth, allowing him to breathe as he ascended. It had spared John's life.

John no longer felt disgusted by the tentacle. His disgust had been replaced with a mixture of relief and gratitude. What had been repulsive only moments before suddenly felt invigorating, and he clung to the feeling. The taste of petrol and rotting fish was now gone and a sweeter, more pleasant taste filled his mouth. John felt more alive than he ever had before. He felt free.

As the god raised John toward the light of the surface he could see that most of the god remained in the dark depths below. John broke the now-calm surface of the water and the god slid its tentacle from John's mouth and silently disappeared back into the abyss below. John felt a moment of disappointment and emptiness.

The god was gone.

John was alone.

The last of St. Budoc's Island had fallen beneath the waves. It had crumbled into the sea to join Atlantis in the realm of sunken cities.

John woke up on a beach somewhere, face down in the sand, with the sun beating down on his skin. He tried to open his eyes to look around but the sun was too bright and his eyelids were stuck together with salt. He rubbed his eyes and tried to open them a crack, squinting as they adjusted to the new light. He looked along the beach. There was debris everywhere. Wrecked ships, clothes, rubble, and the bodies of St. Budoc's inhabitants all littered the beach. The waves gently lapped at John's ankles as he drifted out of consciousness.

TWENTY-THREE

Longevity is the reward of the blessed.
An old Hebridean proverb.

'What about the island?' Anne Jackson asked John Calvary as they sat on the bench in the gardens of Wallace Psychiatric Hospital.

It was almost dark. The sky was painted with beautiful oranges and pinks and the birds were singing their final songs of the day. The mallards swimming on the pond were calling the other ducks before they flew away over the trees to wherever they had built their nests.

Several bats flew overhead as they chased the moths. John watched them fly around the garden and then into the tall trees. The woods that circled the hospital grounds were black inside.

'They put its submergence down to something or other,' John said. He was exhausted. He had told his story only a few times since admitting himself to the hospital, but never in as much detail, and it had drained him. 'I don't remember what they said exactly; an earthquake, an underwater volcano, or something like that. As far as I know there weren't any other survivors from the island who could testify. Not that they would want to now. It was so long ago. And who would even believe them?' He lingered on those last words as he looked at Anne. Did she believe him?

John looked away into the darkening blue sky above the trees in the distance. A single star shone above the tree line.

Venus? John wondered. He used to enjoy stargazing, but now the thought of there being anything larger than himself looming in the vastness of space made him feel uneasy.

'How long ago was this?' Anne asked. 'When did it all happen?'

John laughed as he looked into Anne's eyes.

'What's so funny?' she asked.

John could tell she was as tired as he was and hoped his story had been a welcomed distraction from facing the horrors of Sam's attempted suicide. The nurses said that they'd have to wait until tomorrow to find out if Sam had been successful or not. It was still unclear as to whether or not he would make it. John hoped that he would. He really liked Sam.

'How old do you think I am?' John asked, smiling.

Anne studied his face for a moment before asking, 'Is this a trick question?'

'Just guess.' He chuckled.

'I don't know...' Anne said, trying to figure him out. 'Sixty?' she said and then quickly changed her answer to, 'Seventy?'

John laughed as he shook his head. He liked it when people tried to guess his age. 'I'm not sure I should tell you,' he said.

'Please,' Anne said.

'In about three weeks,' John said, 'I'll have my one hundred and seventh birthday.'

'Shut up,' Anne said and then quickly said. 'Sorry, that was rude. No, how old are you really?'

John laughed again. 'I'm telling you the truth.'

'A hundred and seven?'

John nodded. 'A hundred and seven.'

Anne gasped. 'I never would have guessed, and I almost don't believe you.'

'I wouldn't have expected you to,' John said. 'If you ask nicely, one of the nurses will confirm it.'

'A hundred and seven,' Anne muttered to herself in disbelief. 'You need to tell me what moisturiser you use.'

'Since that day in the sea, I've never been sick. I once sat naked in the snow to see if I'd catch hypothermia.'

'And?'

John shrugged. 'I didn't even catch a cold,' he said. 'During the pandemic, which was long before your time, we lost a lot of good people here. Places like this were hit the worst. At first, I tried to avoid getting sick, just like everyone else. I wore a mask and used hand gel after entering and leaving every room. But there was one week just before the second lockdown where all but ten of us were sick. I stopped washing my hands, I'd speak, unmasked, to the sick but nothing... not even a tickle in my throat. It was the most contagious disease on the planet but it wouldn't come near me.' John shook his head as he remembered. 'That *thing* gave me more than just my life back. It gave me a whole new life entirely.'

'That's incredible,' Anne muttered. 'Do you believe that it really was a god? Or... is a god?' she asked. 'Do you know if it's still alive?'

'Can I ask you something?' John said.

'Sure.'

'Do you believe in the afterlife?' John asked.

'Like in the Bible?' Anne asked.

'I don't know if what I saw was really a god or just pretending to be a god. But I think one of the reasons it kept me alive is because it sympathised with me and it wanted to spare me from the afterlife. Which made me wonder... if that thing *is* a god, and if Kaala was *also* a god, then I don't want to find out what kind of afterlife it might have sent me to; where it might have sent Sarah and Patrick...'

...Or where it might send Sam, if he doesn't make it, John thought, but he didn't share this part with Anne.

Anne's eyes flickered over John's face, as a last attempt to try and suss him out. She didn't know if she should believe him or not, but she tried desperately to figure out if he believed himself. It sounded like he did.

'Do you want to know the real reason that I'm here?' John asked. 'It isn't because of that *thing* I saw, or even because of Patrick and Sarah's deaths. It's because everyone I've ever known and loved has died, and most likely everyone I'm yet to meet will also die, whilst I live on for God-knows how long. And I'm absolutely *terrified* of what kind of afterlife they're in.'

After a while, Anne felt well enough to drive. The receptionist offered to call her a taxi or, if she really wanted to, she could have spent the night in the staff quarters, but Anne told her that she would rather go home. She was shaken but enough time had passed now that she felt that she was okay to drive home by herself. She planned on getting home, making herself a big bowl of pasta to eat in the bath, and cancelling all of her appointments for the next day before going to bed without setting an alarm.

'How are you feeling?' a nurse asked her as she was walking to her car after her shift.

'I've just been talking to John Calvary,' Anne said.

'He's a brave fellow, saving Sam like that,' the nurse said. 'He would have made a great nurse in another life.'

'He told me his story,' Anne said.

The nurse nodded and smiled. 'Yeah, he's told a few of us that story,' she said.

'You don't believe him, do you?' Anne asked.

'I don't want to sound disrespectful,' the nurse said, 'because I really respect John, but we do get a lot of stories in a place like this.' She gestured to the looming psychiatric hospital behind them. 'Mind you, none so vivid or as detailed as his.' The windows of the hospital glowed like dozens of orange eyes in the darkness. 'John suffers from delusions and night terrors and has done so since he was admitted here. Whatever he's told you… just keep that in mind. He's a nice man, but so are a lot of patients here.'

The nurse got into her car and drove away, leaving Anne standing by her car in disappointment. She didn't know if she believed John's story or not, but she knew that she wanted to believe him.

John lay in his bed. His feet barely touched the bottom of the mattress as he lay on top of his covers. He spread his arms out either side of him and stared up at the tiled ceiling. He liked to count the tiles when he couldn't sleep, which was often. There weren't any patterns to find in the ceiling here, so he settled with counting things instead: the tiles, a nurse's steps, his own heartbeats. Sleep was where his nightmares lurked, showing him strange visions of distant, inhuman worlds. Worlds he hoped only existed in his dreams, but he couldn't be sure. Counting tiles was a much better alternative. He hated sleep.

Beside John's bed stood a photo of Sarah in her last year of school. She had sent it to John after she had graduated secondary school, and it was the only photo he had of any of his family. He had almost completely forgotten what his parents had looked like and, as far as he knew, no photos of them existed anymore.

Their photos are sat at the bottom of the sea, with the rest of St. Budoc's Island, John thought. He smiled as he looked at the photo of Sarah. She looked pretty. Her face was the same face he remembered from their last few days together, but her expression was less tired, her eyes more hopeful. He liked to remember her like this.

He opened the drawer in his bedside cabinet and pulled out a bundle of cloth. He unrolled it and took out the Viking spearhead. It was all he had managed to save from the island.

He rotated it in his hands, looking at the intricate patterns carved onto the blade. He remembered the day that he had pulled it out of the creature on West Beach and thought of Lawrence as he turned the spearhead in his hands.

Anne turned the overhead light on inside her car, which dimly illuminated her bag on the seat next to her. Most of the day nurses had gone home and the night nurses had arrived for their shifts. A security guard walked through the car park, shining his torch in front of him. When he saw Anne sitting in her car, he asked if she was okay. She told him that she was fine, and he let her be.

Anne rummaged through her bag and took out her tablet. She turned it on and swiped through her apps until she found the one she was looking for: *Maps*.

She tapped on it. The screen remained blue as it loaded up and then turned green and narrowed in on her current location. She only had a single bar of reception, so everything took a while longer to load than it would normally take at home. She switched the map to the satellite view and saw an aerial view of the ancient trees that surrounded her. The woods were even more vast than she had realised. She could see the roof of the hospital amongst the trees, and behind it she could see the long garden where she and John had spent the whole day sitting together, and where John had told her all about St. Budoc's Island.

Anne tapped the search bar and typed in, 'St. Budoc's Island.' She hit the search button and waited for it to load. The screen turned blue again before the Outer Hebrides finally loaded up. For a second she didn't think it would work.

She zoomed in on the place that was labelled St. Budoc's Island and saw nothing but water.

She sighed. Maybe it was just a tall tale, after all.

Then something caught her eye and she zoomed in on the spot. She turned up the brightness and peered closer, lifting the tablet to her eyes so she could get a better view. The glow from the screen illuminated her face in blue-white light. In the place where St. Budoc's Island should have been was a strange shape lurking underwater. It was huge and dark, like a giant oil slick, and almost the same size as the nearest island.

Anne's brow furrowed and she looked even closer at the shadow beneath the waves. It was large and round, and strange lines trailed from the main body like creeping vines… or tentacles.

The image was low quality and the shape was hard to see, as though it were deep underwater, but there was clearly something there. It was almost impossible to make out what it was, but Anne thought she knew what it might've been.

It might just be a god.

THE END

CHECK OUT OTHER GREAT DEEP SEA THRILLERS

THE BREACH
by **Edward J. McFadden III**

A Category 4 hurricane punched a quarter mile hole in Fire Island, exposing the Great South Bay to the ferocity of the Atlantic Ocean, and the current pulled something terrible through the new breach. A monstrosity of the past mixed with the present has been disturbed and it's found its way into the sheltered waters of Long Island's southern sea.

Nate Tanner lives in Stones Throw, Long Island. A disgraced SCPD detective lieutenant put out to pasture in the marine division because of his Navy background and experience with aquatic crime scenes, Tanner is assigned to hunt the creeper in the bay. But he and his team soon discover they're the ones being hunted.

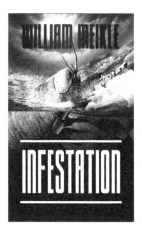

INFESTATION
by **William Meikle**

It was supposed to be a simple mission. A suspected Russian spy boat is in trouble in Canadian waters. Investigate and report are the orders.

But when Captain John Banks and his squad arrive, it is to find an empty vessel, and a scene of bloody mayhem.

Soon they are in a fight for their lives, for there are things in the icy seas off Baffin Island, scuttling, hungry things with a taste for human flesh.

They are swarming. And they are growing.

"Scotland's best Horror writer" - Ginger Nuts of Horror

"The premier storyteller of our time." - Famous Monsters of Filmland

Check out other great

Sea Monster Novels!

Michael Cole

CREATURE OF LAKE SHADOW

It was supposed to be a simple bank robbery. Quick. Clean. Efficient. It was none of those. With police searching for them across the state, a band of criminals hide out in a desolate cabin on the frozen shore of Lake Shadow. Isolated, shrouded in thick forest, and haunted by a mysterious history, they thought it was the perfect place to hide. Tensions mount as they hear strange noises outside. Slain animals are found in the snow. Before long, they realize something is watching them. Something hungry, violent, and not of this world. In their attempt to escape, they found the Creature of Lake Shadow.

Matt James

SUB-ZERO

The only thing colder than the Antarctic air is the icy chill of death... Off the coast of McMurdo Station, in the frigid waters of the Southern Ocean, a new species of Antarctic octopus is unintentionally discovered. Specialists aboard a state-of-the-art DARPA research vessel aim to apply the animal's "sub-zero venom" to one of their projects: An experimental painkiller designed for soldiers on the front lines. All is going according to plan until the ship is caught in an intense storm. The retrofitted tanker is rocked, and the onboard laboratory is destroyed. Amid the chaos, the lead scientist is infected by a strange virus while conducting the specimen's dissection. The scientist didn't die in the accident. He changed.

CHECK OUT OTHER GREAT DEEP SEA THRILLERS

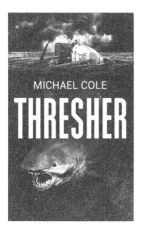

THRESHER
by Michael Cole

In the aftermath of a hurricane, a series of strange events plague the coastal waters off Florida. People go into the water and never return. Corpses of killer whales drift ashore, ravaged from enormous bite marks. A fishing trawler is found adrift, with a mysterious gash in its hull.

Transferred to the coastal town of Merit, police officer Leonard Riker uncovers the horrible reality of an enormous Thresher shark lurking off the coast. Forty feet in length, it has taken a territorial claim to the waters near the town harbor. Armed with three-inch teeth, a scythe-like caudal fin, and unmatched aggression, the beast seeks to kill anything sharing the waters.

THE GUILLOTINE
by Lucas Pederson

1,000 feet under the surface, Prehistoric Anthropologist, Ash Barrington, and his team are in the midst of a great archeological dig at the bottom of Lake Superior where they find a treasure trove of bones. Bones of dinosaurs that aren't supposed to be in this particular region. In their underwater facility, Infinity Moon, Ash and his team soon discover a series of underground tunnels. Upon exploring, they accidentally open an ice pocket, thawing the prehistoric creature trapped inside. Soon they are being attacked, the facility falling apart around them, by what Ash knows is a dunkleosteus and all those bones were from its prey. Now...Ash and his team are the prey and the creature will stop at nothing to get to them.

Made in the USA
Coppell, TX
29 March 2023

14941653R00095